ALSO BY DANITA CARTER
Murder in the Hamptons

peer
pleasure

DANITA CARTER

SBI

STREBOR BOOKS

NEW YORK LONDON TORONTO SYDNEY

SBl

Strebor Books
P.O. Box 6505
Largo, MD 20792
http://www.streborbooks.com

ISBN 978-1-59309-251-1
ISBN 978-1-4165-9704-9 (e-book)
LCCN 2010925101

First Strebor Books trade paperback edition April 2009

Cover design: www.mariondesigns.com
Cover photograph: © Keith Saunders/Marion Designs

10 9 8 7 6 5 4 3 2 1

Manufactured in the United States of America

For information regarding special discounts for bulk purchases,
please contact Simon & Schuster Special Sales at 1-866-506-1949
or business@simonandschuster.com

The Simon & Schuster Speakers Bureau can bring authors to your
live event. For more information or to book an event, contact the
Simon & Schuster Speakers Bureau at 1-866-248-3049 or visit our
website at www.simonspeakers.com.

I DEDICATE THIS BOOK TO MY MOTHER, ALLINE CARTER,
who has believed in my artistic abilities
my entire life (even before I knew I had
any "artistic abilities"…LOL).
Mom, I love you with all my heart!!!
Danita

acknowledgments

Peer Pleasure has been a "pleasure" to write, (pun intended!), but it would not have been possible without the following people...

My agent, Sara Camilli, you are simply put—The BEST!!! Thank you for shopping *Peer Pleasure* until we got the deal!!!

Zane, I want to thank you for recognizing a good story, when you read one!!

Charmaine Parker, Publishing Director, Strebor Books, thank you for keeping me on track along the way.

And to the young people in my life who keep me abreast of what's happening...

My nephews, Ronald Carter II, Daniel Carter, Khary Milloy, Quinton Woodward, Evan Woodward, Xavier Tillman, and Graham Lucas.

My nieces, Danique Carter, Iman Carter, and Tamiia Carter. And to my goddaughter, Britany Russell. For my other godchildren, don't get mad, but you're too young to read this book yet, so I'll have to write another one just for you guys!!

And to the readers...Never give in to *Peer Pleasure!!!*

Much Love,

Danita

1

"We're here at Seventh on Sixth, the seasonal industry fashion show. As you can see—" the reporter turned slightly to her left to let the cameraman get a better angle, "—the giant white tents are pitched high in Bryant Park where the actual shows are taking place. Inside, strutting the catwalk, is Seventh Avenue's latest sensation, Madison Reynolds. Though only sixteen, Madison has more poise than models twice her age," the entertainment reporter spoke into the camera.

There seemed to be a small village of reporters from around the globe staked out in front of Bryant Park, as well as an army of photographers inside. New York Fashion Week was a huge deal and they were there to report not only on the latest designers, but also on the fashion world's next ingénue.

The reporter continued, "Despite her mile-long legs, flawless skin, flowing red hair and emerald-green eyes, Madison would be just another wannabe model if it weren't for her grandmother, Renée Reynolds. A top model back in the days of Janice Dickinson and Beverly Johnson, Renée still has a foothold in the industry and has used her connections to get Madison through a few tightly closed doors."

The reporter was trying to fill up the time until Madison came out of the show, so she gave a little background information on Madison's ever-present grandmother. After nearly an hour, the opening of the entrance tent parted and out pranced the models.

"Madison! Madison, over here!" shouted the reporter, as she exited the tent.

"Quick! Snap her picture! Snap her picture!" the reporter instructed her photographer.

Madison stopped on the red carpet and struck a haughty pose, but before she could flash her signature smile, another photog called her name. She swiveled around on her (mucho mature) Manolos and turned, with smile in place, while the photographer clicked away.

"So, Madison, when's your next gig?" asked the inquiring reporter.

"I'll be doing the spring shows in Paris," Madison answered with a smile.

"Which houses are you modeling for this year?"

"I'll be doing the rounds as usual." Though she was a teen, Madison was a regular on the European circuit.

"What about school? Are you taking a semester off, or are you going to get a tutor?"

"I uhh…"

Before she could answer, her ever-present grand-mother chimed in. "Come on, honey," she said, tugging on Madison's arm, "that's enough press for one evening."

"Renée, will you be accompanying your granddaughter to Europe?" the reporter asked, trying to prolong her time with the Reynolds women.

Renée arched her back and cleared her throat. "Of course. Let's not forget that not too long ago, I worked those same shows," she said with an air of indignation.

"How could anyone ever forget the Renée Reynolds strut? You had a walk like no other," the reporter said, stroking the older woman's obviously fragile ego. The reporter thought that if she could get next to Madison's bulldog of a grandmother, then maybe she'd get an exclusive interview with the young model. But before she could ask another question, another group of models came pouring onto the red carpet.

"Madison, are you going to meet us at the Gansevoort?" asked Danielle, a fellow model.

Madison wanted to go and hang out with the other girls, but she knew that was out of the question. There was no way her grandmother was going to let her go to the Meatpacking District and party at the trendy boutique hotel. Madison didn't want to sound like the underaged teen that she was, so she simply said, "No, I've got an early day tomorrow."

"Oh, do you have an early morning shoot?" Danielle asked.

"Nah." In model lingo, an early day usually meant a nine o'clock shoot, but for Madison it meant that she had to get up early and go to school—high school, not college.

Madison attended Walburton Academy, one of Manhattan's premier private schools on the Upper West Side. While the schools on the East Side educated mostly blue-blooded, old-money brats, the West Side institutions were filled with a cornucopia of first- and second-generation wealth. Being a top teen model, Madison reigned supreme over her crew of four. There was her best friend and partner in shopping, Reagan. Reagan's biggest fan and admirer, former child star Peyton Granger, better known as PG, and Ian, Madison's boyfriend. Though it could be grueling at times, Madison loved her school. It was one of the few places where she could let loose and have some fun without the prying eyes of the paparazzi *or* her grandmother.

"Are you sure you don't want to go? 'Cuz we gonna party like rock stars." Danielle laughed and slapped her friend a high-five, ready to get the night started.

Madison quickly looked at her grandmother, who had a scowl plastered across her face. Obviously she wasn't happy with this verbal exchange.

"Yeah, I'm sure. You guys have fun. I'll hang out with you at the next gig," Madison said, trying to sound like an adult instead of a curfew-reddened teenager.

"Alright. See ya when I see ya," Danielle said, then

waved her hand and got into a waiting limo with her entourage.

Madison threw her hand up and said good-bye as she followed her grandmother to their car. She couldn't wait until she was old enough to party without a chaperone. The way her grandmother watched her so closely, Madison felt like a specimen underneath a microscope.

"We're going to take my granddaughter home first," Renée instructed her driver once they were settled in the back of her sleek black-on-black Jaguar XJ8.

The driver nodded without saying a word, and took off up Sixth Avenue. Madison lived with her parents and little brother on Sixty-eighth and Central Park West, in a renovated, pre-war, three-bedroom coop. Her mother—who didn't inherit the leggy model body—was a housewife, and her father was an investment banker for Morgan Stanley. Her parents rarely attended the fashion shows, since her dad was at client dinners most nights and her mother was devoted to Madison's baby brother, Henry. So the job of overseer naturally went to her grandmother.

"You did a good job tonight, honey," Renée said.

"Thanks."

"Except…"

Oh here it comes, Madison thought. Her grandmother's compliments were usually followed by detailed criticism.

"…when you turn at the end of the runway, pause a little longer so that the photographer can get a chance to snap your picture. Tonight, you turned too fast, and even if he did take a shot, I'm sure he only got the back of your head."

"Okay," was all that Madison said. She was used to the instruction, and let it go in one ear and out the other. She knew that her grandmother had good intentions, but at times she really wasn't in the mood for the critique.

Luckily for Madison, her Sidekick vibrated inside her Dooney bag before the rhetoric continued. She dug into the oversized duffel and fished out her metallic silver connection to the world. She flipped open the screen and saw that she had a text from Reagan. She punched a few keys and read the message:

i got sme grt nws!

Madison quickly typed a short reply on the mini keyboard:

cant tlk. wcyl

She pressed send, closed the phone, and put it back in her bag. From the corner of her eye, Madison could see her grandmother looking over at her. The last thing she needed was for her grandmother to try and decode one of her texts. If her grandmother had seen the message, she'd be full of questions like the freaking Gestapo. First off, she'd want to know who the message was from, and second she'd want to know what "wcyl" stood for. Madison smiled slightly when she realized that even if her grandmother had seen the message, she'd never guess that "wcyl" meant "will call you later." Now that she thought about it, texting was a totally safe mode of communication in front of mostly any adult, since they were oblivious to the encrypted language of texting.

"Who was that calling you so late?"

Here comes the interrogation, Madison thought. "It wasn't a call, Nancy." Renée had insisted that her grandchildren call her Nancy, a derivate of Nana. In her mind, she was too young to be called Grandma, and Nana was more befitting of a booty-knitting, cookie-baking grandmother, which she certainly was not. And when Madison called her Nancy at industry functions, she felt like a hip, older aunt, instead of a relic.

"You know what I mean." She pinned Madison with one of her "don't be a smarty pants" looks.

"That was Reagan reminding me that we have a field trip tomorrow," she lied. It wasn't exactly a lie since their class was scheduled to attend a Broadway matinee.

"Oh," Renée said, satisfied with the answer. She knew that she was being overprotective at times, but didn't want her granddaughter to grow up too fast. Modeling was a cutthroat business, a business where young girls were used and abused on a regular basis. And it was her responsibility to make sure that Madison didn't get involved with alcohol, drugs or grown men looking for a ripe young virgin.

Before the interrogation could continue, the car was pulling up in front of Madison's building. She was glad to escape the prying eyes of her grandmother, and couldn't wait to be alone in her room, so that she could answer Reagan's text freely.

"Good night, Nancy." Madison pecked her grandmother on the cheek. "Thanks for dropping me off."

"Anytime, my darling." She gave Madison a tight hug. "Now get some rest, and I'll talk to you soon."

"I will, and thanks for coming with me tonight." Even though Madison resented her grandmother's presence at times, a part of her was actually glad that she was there to run interference with the groupies that she didn't want to be bothered with.

"Hey, Sam," Madison greeted the doorman once she was inside the building.

"Good evening, Miss. Another late night, I see."

"Yeah, I was modeling in a fashion show tonight."

"I don't know where you get the energy, between school and your modeling career. It's a wonder you don't have dark circles under your eyes."

"Trust me, Sam, I make up on my sleep time on the weekends. Besides, I'm young and can handle the pressure." She chuckled. "Good night."

"Good night, Miss."

Madison rode the elevator up to her family's apartment. She quietly opened the door. The apartment was dim, with only one lamp on in the living room. Madison didn't hear her noisy little brother bouncing around, which could only mean that he was asleep, which meant that her mother was also alseep, since she mirrored her son's sleep pattern. Madison was grateful for the peace and quiet, because the only person she wanted to talk to was Reagan. She made a beeline for her bedroom and immediately called her best friend.

"It's about time," Reagan whispered into the phone. "I've been on pins and needles waiting for your call."

"You know I couldn't talk with Nancy listening to my every word. What's up?"

"You know that stupid field trip we're going on tomorrow?"

"Yeah, what about it?"

"Well…" Reagan paused for effect. "We're not going!" she shrieked softly.

Madison kicked off her heels, sat on the bed and rubbed her aching toes. The high heels were cute, but not the most comfortable shoes. "Why? Was it cancelled?"

"You could say that," Reagan said mysteriously.

"Come on, Rea, stop teasing, and tell me what the heck you're talking about."

"PG called earlier this evening and told me that Ian's parents are going to their house in the Hamptons in the morning, so that they can attend some film festival. And Ian will have the penthouse all to himself for the next few days. So instead of going to some stupid play, me, you and PG are spending the afternoon at Ian's!" she whispered excitedly.

"That's awesome! I could use some down time after working and being spied on all evening. I love my grand-mother to death, but I swear sometimes she drives me crazy; acting like my private bodyguard."

"Ms. Thang, you don't have to worry about prying eyes tomorrow, because the only people at the penthouse will be us. Ian's going to send the maid out for the day, so we can really cut up!"

"Now that's the kind of field trip I'm talkin' about! No teachers, no parents *or* grandparents, and no nosey housekeepers! Party over here, ooh, ooh," Madison sang out in a soft tone, so that she wouldn't wake her mother.

"Okay! Girl, I can't wait. Tomorrow can't come fast enough."

"I love Ian's absentee parents. They care more about socializing than staying at home looking after their kid, unlike my mom, who's always at the house with me and my brother," Madison said.

"I saw Ian's parents in the society section of *The Times* last week, photographed at some party with the mayor."

"Ian's left alone so much, it's like he's an orphan."

"An orphan with a fabu penthouse, don't forget!" Reagan laughed.

"This is true."

"Wait a minute." Reagan paused for a second. "I think I hear my mom walking down the hall. Unlike Ian's mom, mine is on constant patrol. Let me go before she comes storming in here, snatches the phone out of my hand, and demands I go to bed."

"Okay, I'll see you tomorrow." Madison hung up. With visions of a stress-free afternoon lying ahead, Madison danced around her room in her bare feet, anticipating a day of unsupervised fun with her friends.

2

"**M**agdala, I need for you to run some errands for me today," Ian addressed the housekeeper as he came out of his bedroom.

"Mr. Ian, I have work to do for you mother," she said, holding an arm full of clothes. "Before she left, Señora instruct me to take these things to cleaners, and then…"

He cut her off. "Magdala, you can drop them off on your way to the Bronx."

"BRONX!" She bucked her eyes, and raised her voice. "Me no go to Bronx." She shook her head back and forth.

Ian handed her a season schedule for the Yankees, with red circles around two dates. "I want four tickets to these games," he said, pointing to the outlines.

"Me no can go," she said, still protesting.

"Yes, you can, and just for doing me this favor, I'm going to also buy you two tickets," he said, softening the negotiation.

Magdala smiled. Her husband was a huge Yankees fan, and would flip over seeing the game live. "Oh…" Her eyes bucked wide again, but this time in delight. "Okay. Okay, Mr. Ian." She grinned.

"Good. Then, I'll need for you to take the train to Brooklyn, and stop by Cake Man Raven's bakery on Fulton Street and pick up a red velvet cake."

"BROOKLYN!" Her grin quickly disappeared. Clearly she didn't want to go from one borough to the next. "No, no, Mr. Ian. Too much; too many trains," she said, shaking her head. "Me supposed to be here with you, not on train."

"That's silly. I'm not a baby. Besides, I'll be in school all day." Ian reached into his pocket and took out his wallet—which was always stocked full of cash—and handed her three crisp one-hundred dollar bills. "Here, and keep the change," he said, knowing that money talked louder than words.

Magdala took the money, and slid the bills into the pocket of her apron. "This between me and you, no?" she asked, nodding her head up and down.

"Don't worry. I won't say a word." Ian put his index finger to his mouth and made a *sshh* sound.

Magdala scurried down the hall with her loot. Ian went back into his room, grabbed his backpack, and headed out the door for school. With his unofficial overseer out of the house, traveling through three of New York's boroughs for the better part of the day, Ian figured that he and his friends had at least a few hours of uninterrupted fun, which was more than enough time. Once he got the word that his parents were off to the Hamptons for the annual International Film Festival, he wasted no time hooking up a little get-together. It was perfect timing. Their class was scheduled for a field trip, but instead of seeing a Broadway show, he and his friends would be spending the afternoon at his penthouse.

"I certainly hope that everyone has brought their permission slips for today's field trip," said Mrs. Carey, the fine arts teacher, as she led the class out of the building.

"Mine is right here," Ian patted the breast pocket of his school's monogrammed blazer, "forged by yours personally." He laughed underneath his breath.

"I bet you've been signing your mother's name since before you could spell," PG remarked.

"And I bet you've been signing autographs since you were in pre-school," Ian shot back, making a dig about Payton's former career as a child television star.

"Now, now, boys, let's not bicker," Reagan chimed in.

"Oh, Rea, why stop the fun? They've only just begun," Madison said.

Reagan, Madison, Ian and PG were in line with the rest of their class, walking to the waiting bus outside of their school.

"Slip, please," Mrs. Carey said to Ian before he boarded.

"Here you go, Mrs. Carey," he said, ever so politely, with a fake smile.

She glanced at the signature, and didn't even notice

the forgery. She stood at the entry to the bus, and repeated this protocol until every single student had handed over his or her permission slip and was on board.

"So how are we going to get from the theatre to your place?" Madison whispered in Ian's ear once they were seated on the bus.

"Don't you worry your head about that, 'My Pretty.'" He smirked, using the phrase from *The Wizard of Oz*.

"I don't care how we get there, as long as we're back at the theater before the buses leave. The last thing I need is for my mother to find out that I skipped school," Reagan said.

"Yeah, I know what you mean. If Nancy knew I was escaping for a few hours, she'd have me fitted with an ankle bracelet. And, no, not the decorative kind, the gross kind that people wear when they're under house arrest," Madison commented.

"You're right about that! Your grandmother is the strictest person I know," Ian said.

"She's not that bad. You're not used to answering to anyone since your parents are never around," Madison said, coming to her grandmother's defense.

Ian hung his head, as if Madison had hurt his feelings. "You've got a point," he said, picking his head off of his chest. "My parents are definitely not the warm and fuzzy type, but I like it like that. At least I don't have to worry about them hovering over me on a daily basis. Besides, where else would we hang out if they were always at home?" Ian said, with an air of cockiness, but deep down inside he felt conflicted. On the one hand, Ian did enjoy having the freedom to go and come as he pleased, but on the other hand, he secretly longed for some parental supervision. If his parents were around the house more, he'd probably be inclined to keep out of trouble, but as it were he was his own gatekeeper, and the gate swung nearly off its hinges on any given day.

"Point taken."

They continued chatting, and before long the bus was pulling up in front of the Astor Theatre. While the students filed into the lobby of the auditorium, Reagan, Madison, Ian and PG hung back, and huddled close together, so as not to be separated.

"Before you're seated, please turn off all cell phones, and any other electronic devices that you may have. We don't want to interrupt the show with those annoying little gadgets. No loud gum chewing. And absolutely NO TALKING!" Mrs. Carey emphasized, spouting off a list of "do's and don'ts" of proper theater etiquette.

While the rest of the student body took out their phones and turned them off, Ian took his out, dialed the car service and confirmed his pick-up location.

"Yes, Mr. Reinhardt, your car is waiting right outside. It's car number twenty-three."

"Thank you," Ian said in a hushed tone, and quickly clicked the phone off before the teacher caught him.

"Okay, now that we're clear on how to act at a Broadway

show, you may take your seats," Mrs. Carey said, leading the way into the theater.

Ian, Reagan, Madison and PG brought up the rear of the line, but lagged behind. Once Mrs. Carey and everyone else had settled into their seats and the house lights dimmed, the four of them quickly did an about face and snuck out the front door, right into the waiting Town Car.

"Now that Mrs. Carey has seen us, and collected our permission slips, we won't be reported MIA, even if we are MIA!" Ian laughed.

"Aren't you the clever one?" Madison said.

"I hope you scheduled the car to pick us up before the play is over," Reagan said.

"We'll be in the lobby before the final curtain falls," Ian said, full of himself. He was proud that he had orchestrated their escape.

Once the car pulled in front of Ian's massive apartment building, they all piled out and made a beeline toward the bank of elevators.

"Come on in, guys," Ian said, opening the door to his family's palatial penthouse in the Time Warner Center.

"I love this view," Reagan said, walking over to the triple-paned window. The floor-to-ceiling windows offered spectacular panoramic views of Central Park to the northeast, and the Hudson River to the west. "I only live a few blocks from here, but our view is nothing like this. About all I can see from my place is a little piece of the park." Reagan walked away from the window, and took a tour of the living room. "I love your place. Every time I come over, it's almost like the first time." She lightly ran her hand across the bottom of the huge flat-screen plasma Bang & Olufsen that was mounted on the wall. "I've been trying to get my dad to buy one of these, but he's such a cheapskate, and says it's a waste of money."

"Obviously, he's never seen the picture quality from one of these babies," Ian said proudly, as if he'd forked over the credit card to pay for the extravagant television.

"You're right. I love it," she said, rubbing her hand once again across the smooth surface.

"And I love how your legs look in those shoes," PG commented, leering at Reagan from behind.

"Thanks. They're the new Juicy Couture wedges. Just because we have to wear these boring navy-and-gray uniforms doesn't mean we can't trick 'em out with some bad kicks. Isn't that right, Madison?"

"Totally. I bought these Marc Jacobs the other day," she said, extending the midnight-blue, round-toed shoe for emphasis.

PG focused his attention back on Reagan. "And I love how you pull the knee-socks up past your knees. It's such a sexy look, especially with the school sweater tied around your waist," he said, pouring on the compliments.

Reagan ignored Peyton's comment. She was immune to his constant compliments. It was no big secret that PG had a gargantuan crush on her. He made it known every chance he got that he worshiped Reagan. PG, with his lanky, muscle-less frame and pimpled face wasn't her type, but she tolerated him anyway. Reagan may not have been in love with PG, but she was in love with the expensive gifts that he showered her with. Peyton Granger had been the lead actor in *Little Buddies*, one of the top-rated sitcoms of the mid-nineties. Though he hadn't worked in over ten years, he still raked in the royalty checks, thanks to the reruns on Nickelodeon five nights a week.

PG walked up to Reagan, so close that she could feel his hot breath on her face as he spoke. "Thought you might like this," he said, handing her a robin's egg-blue Tiffany's box.

"PG, what's this?" she asked, fingering the white ribbon tied neatly around the small box.

"Open it and see."

Reagan pulled the ribbon loose and lifted the lid. Inside was a beautiful eighteen-karat, white-gold Atlas lariat with the Roman numerals, twelve, three, six, and nine surrounding a circle of pave diamonds. "Oh, PG, you shouldn't have." She took the necklace out of the box and held it up to the light. "But I'm so glad you did."

"It was a tad spendy, but you're worth every dime," he said, making sure she knew that the gift-du-jour was expensive.

Reagan didn't say a word, she ignored his tacky comment. She hated it when PG alluded to how much money he spent, as if he were broke.

"Here, let me put it on you." He took the necklace out of her hands, lifted her hair and secured the clasp. Once the necklace was fastened, he let his hands linger on her shoulder blades, then leaned down and kissed the side of her neck.

Reagan swung around. "PG, what the hell do you think you're doing?" she asked, pulling away from him.

"Just trying to get a little thank you kiss." He blushed shyly.

"A verbal *thank you* will have to do, 'cause I ain't kissing you today, and I don't want you kissing on me," she said, and huffed away.

"Who wants a Red Bull and Belvedere?" Ian asked, breaking the tension in the room.

"I do," Madison said, followed by Reagan and PG.

Ian retreated into the kitchen, and came back with four cans of the energy drink. He sat the blue-and-silver cans on the bar in the living room, filled four tall glasses with ice, double shots of vodka, and then poured in the Red Bull until it reached the top of each glass. "To field trips," he said, handing each of his friends a glass of the potent beverage. They clinked glasses and toasted. The guys gulped their drinks, while the girls sipped politely.

"Turn on some music. I wanna dance," Madison told Ian.

Ian picked up the remote that was sitting on the bar, clicked it in the direction of the wall mounted B&O stereo, and within seconds, the sound of an old Black Eyed Peas tune filled the room.

"What you gonna do with all that junk inside your trunk…?" Ian sang in unison with the song and danced up close to Madison.

"I'm, I'm, I'm gonna get you drunk…" she sang back, wrapping her arms around his neck.

Reagan felt a twinge of jealousy surge through her body as she watched Madison and Ian gyrate to the music. Madison seemed to enjoy his touch, as his hands roamed up and down her back. They made such a cute couple, and Reagan wanted to be one-half of a pair more than anything else. PG wasn't a serious contender; he was somebody to pass the time with, but he'd have to do until she met her soul mate.

"Do you guys need anything else?" Ian asked.

"No, we're cool," PG said, taking a sip of his drink.

"In that case, we'll be back in a few," Ian said, taking Madison by the hand.

"Don't be too long; remember we have to get back before the play is over," Reagan said, her *frienvy* continuing to grow as Ian and Madison disappeared into his room.

"So, why didn't you let me kiss you earlier?" PG asked Reagan. "I know it's not because you and Madison are so pure." He nodded his head in the direction of Ian's bedroom.

"'Cause you ain't my man," she said, sucking her lips.

"I know I ain't your man, but I'm trying to be," he confessed. "Why do you think I keep giving you these extravagant gifts?"

"'Cause you're generous?"

"Yeah, I'm generous, but I ain't no fool. Now don't get me wrong; I'm crazy about you, Reagan, but I can't keep holding on forever."

"Don't be silly, PG. I don't think you're a fool." Reagan walked over and gave him a quick peck on the lips. She was trying to appease PG. Though she wasn't *into him* into him, she didn't want to lose her generous gifts.

"Wow, a kiss!" He put his hand to his mouth in mock surprise. "What made you change your mind?"

"I don't get it. Either you're complaining when I'm not kissing you, or complaining that I am kissing you. Make up your mind!" Reagan said, seemingly annoyed at him.

"No, no, I'm not complaining. Trust me. I'll take whatever I can get."

"Good. Now shut up, and let's dance."

About twenty minutes later, Madison and Ian reappeared. "Girl, what happened to your hair?" Reagan asked, pointing to Madison's tousled hair.

Madison quickly ran her hand over her unruly tresses. "What are you talking about? My hair is fine."

"But your blouse isn't." Reagan walked closer, and tugged at her friend's top. "Since when did you start using the wrong button holes?"

Madison pulled away. "Stop being all in my business." She gave Reagan a look that read, '*You know good and well what I was doing.*'

"Okay, okay, I can take a hint. We'd better get back to the theater before we get busted," Madison said, ready to leave.

"Yeah, you're right. Come on, guys," Ian said. "I told the driver to wait. He should still be downstairs."

They filed out, and once inside of the limo, Reagan couldn't help but to think again how much she wanted a real relationship of her own, not like the buddy-buddy thing she had going on with PG. But until she met someone new, who was fine *and* generous, PG would just have to do.

3

"T"hat was good, Lucas, but let's try it again from the top," said Kevin Myers, the CEO of Heavy-Tone Records, sitting behind the mammoth control panel in the recording studio.

Lucas readjusted his headphones, and started singing again.

"Man, where'd you get this kid from?" asked Mike, the recording engineer. "Not only can he rap like Jay-Z and 50 Cent, he sings like Mario and Justin."

"Believe it or not, I found him at a high school talent show."

"Talent show? You've got to be kidding me!" Mike said, unable to believe that such a talent was performing in such an amateur event.

"Yeah, I was there to see my nephew who was one of the acts. He was okay, but when Lucas stepped on stage and started rapping, an original song I might add, I had to sign him."

"You signed him on the spot?"

"No, it took three months of schmoozing his mother

to convince her to let her son become an HeavyTone artist. At first she thought I was full of it, but when I took her on a tour of our studios, showed her our roster of stars, and a contract with a mid six-figure advance, she said okay, but only if it didn't interfere with his school work."

"Money talks."

"Yeah, Man, it surely does, especially for a single mother living in a cramped one-bedroom apartment with a growing teenager."

"Where's his father?"

"Lucas' mom, Peggy, didn't really get into the details. She just said that Lucas' dad passed away when Lucas was a baby," Kevin said.

"What did he die from?"

"She didn't really say, but I get the feeling that his death was sudden."

"Man, that's a tough break." Mike shook his head.

"Yeah, it is, but their days of struggling are over. Mark my words; Lucas Williams is going to be a mega-star." Kevin smiled as he watched Lucas belt out the lyrics.

"Turn around, baby, and let me hit dat thang, hit dat thang," Lucas sang into the microphone. He was in the recording booth, in his own world. As he bopped his head to the beat, huge locks of his curly hair bounced up and down in sync with the music.

"Look at this kid. Not only can he perform, he's a lady-killer. The girls are going to go crazy over his toned, tall, athletic physique, and they're going to lose their minds over his hazel eyes," Kevin said proudly as if he were Lucas' dad.

"Yeah, he does have an exotic look. His skin is almost the color of a penny; looks like he's been lying on a tropical beach. Actually, he looks more like one of those Gap models, instead of a singer."

"And that's a good thing. At least we won't have to spend a fortune overhauling his looks like some of our other artists. I tell you, Lucas is definitely a natural."

"Once I wrap my charms around ya, ya gonna be beggin' me to take dat thang, take dat thang," Lucas continued.

The speakers in the recording studio were turned up loud and Kevin and Mike bopped their heads to the beat. "Who wrote the lyrics to this song?" Mike asked.

"Lucas did."

"Don't you think they're a little provocative for a boy his age? I mean, he's talking about getting a girl into bed."

"Naw, Man, that's what the kids these days listen to."

"Yeah, I guess you're right. Do you think Lucas has had sex yet?" Mike asked out of curiosity.

"I doubt it. Man, he's only sixteen. He hasn't even mentioned having a girlfriend. Besides, his mom is so overprotective, I'm sure she monitors her son's every move."

"Actually, that's a good thing, because once you're toast, you can never be bread again," Mike said.

"What does that mean?" Kevin asked.

"It means that once you give up your virginity, you can't get it back. Like you can't un-toast bread; once it pops up out of the toaster, it's a done deal."

"I never heard that analogy before. But you're right, once you do the deed, it's most definitely a done deal. Lucas is a smart kid, and I'm sure he won't get into anything too heavy before he's ready. At least I hope not. I got plans for this kid, and it doesn't include fatherhood before his eighteenth birthday," Kevin said, sounding again like Lucas' dad.

After hours of recording and re-recording, Kevin called it a wrap for the day. "Looks like we'll be finished with the first single by next week," he told Lucas once he stepped out of the recording booth.

Lucas smiled broadly, exposing his perfectly white grill. "Man, that's quick."

"That's because I'm working with top-notch talent." Kevin slapped Lucas on the shoulder.

"When are we going to start shooting the video?" Lucas asked anxiously.

"I was going to schedule production in a few weeks, but I think we should wait. After all, you're recording *and* going to school at the same time. Maybe we should wait until you have a break so you'll have more time to focus on the project."

"I can focus just fine. Besides, I'd rather shoot the video as soon as possible so we can get some airplay on

MTV and BET. We both know a record ain't nothin' without a slammin' video," Lucas said firmly, sounding like a true mogul in the making.

Kevin had been in the business for a long time, and over the years he'd seen his fair share of wannabe musicians who were not willing to do the work to produce a hit record—all they wanted to do was party—but this kid seemed to instinctively know what it took to become a star.

"I know. I know." Kevin chuckled as he listened to Lucas dispensing advice.

Lucas thought for a second, trying to come up with a solution. "I got an idea!" He beamed. "I'll beg my mom to let me have a few days off before I start my new school," he said, with hope gleaming in his eyes.

"Now that sounds like a plan, but why are you starting a new school?" Mike asked, chiming in.

"We're moving to the West Side, and my mom insists that I go to Walburton Academy," he said, with a hint of disdain in his voice.

"Why are you sounding like she's shipping you off to boarding school? Walburton Academy is extremely prestigious. It's one of the best private schools in the city," Kevin told him.

"Yeah, I know. But I like my old school just fine," Lucas said, digging his hands deep into the front pockets of his jeans.

"It might be fine, but it's not a top-notch college preparatory high school. I'm sure your mother only wants you to have the best education that you can possibly have," Kevin said knowingly.

"Yeah, that's what she said."

"Do you think your mom will go for you taking a few days off?" Kevin asked skeptically.

"I sure hope so, 'cause I'm not looking forward to going to that uppity school anyway. The longer I delay facing all those stuck-up brats, the better."

"You think it's that uppity?"

"No doubt," Lucas huffed. "Don't nothing but rich kids go to private schools, and I ain't grow up like that." All of his life Lucas had watched his mother struggle to pay the rent, put food on the table, and clothes on their backs. Like most of the kids in his neighborhood, he was accustomed to living the simple life.

"You're a rich kid now, and will be *extremely* rich very soon," Kevin reminded him.

"Man, you know what I mean. Them kids at Walburton ain't just a few hundred thousand rich. They's a few hundred million rich, even a billion, with *ooolllddd* money," he said, stretching out the word *old*.

"I know exactly what you're talking about, and trust me, you're going to be a multi-millionaire before you graduate high school," Kevin assured him.

Lucas blushed. "You think so?"

"I know so!" Kevin smiled. "I've been in the business longer than you've been on this earth, and I know a star when I see one. You got the looks, the talent and the smarts. If you stick with my plan, you'll be on *Billboard*'s Top Ten by next year."

"Even if that happens, I never want to forget where I come from," Lucas said with sincerity.

"That's good to hear. I'm glad you're grounded, because you're going to have so many screaming chicks after you that you're going to have to hire a personal bodyguard to keep them off of you."

"I'ma stay grounded, 'cause that's who I am. But, on the other hand, I do like the sound of girls screaming my name," he said, sounding like the sixteen-year-old that he was.

"And why is that?"

"'Cuz I ain't never had a serious girlfriend. It seems like every girl I liked always liked someone else, and if they liked me, I wasn't into them."

"Trust me, once your CD and video drops, all that's going to change. Remember that some girls will like you because you're a star, and some will genuinely like you as a person."

"How will I know the difference?"

"Now, that'll be tough. But you'll be able to spot the little money-grubbers a mile away, because those will be the ones who'll want expensive gifts and free tickets to every concert so they can tag along with you like groupies. On the other hand, a girl that's truly interested in you, will care less about your fame, and more about you as an individual, and not a brand," Kevin said, giving some wise advice.

"I'll keep that in mind," Lucas said, paying close attention to Kevin's words. He had the career of his dreams; maybe now he could finally meet the girl of his dreams.

"Come on, man, let me take you home, and have a chat with your mother about shooting the video before you start the new school."

"Okay, sounds good."

"See ya, Mike," Kevin said, as the two bounced out of the studio, hopped into a taxi and headed uptown to plead with the *boss*.

4

"Mom, I'm home," Lucas called out once he and Kevin entered the small cramped apartment. "Have a seat, if you can find one. My mom's been packing for days, and has boxes all over the furniture."

Kevin picked up a small box, removed it from the sofa, and sat down. "When are you guys moving?"

"Next week. I'll be right back. Let me see if she's in my bedroom packing," Lucas said, excusing himself. A few seconds later, he came back into the living room. "She's not here. She must have stepped out. You want something to drink?"

"Sure. What you got?"

Lucas walked into the tiny kitchen adjacent to the living room and opened the fridge. "Let's see. There's milk, orange juice, and ginger ale."

"Can you make me a mix?"

"Man, don't tell me you like OJ and ginger ale mixed together?"

"Yep, sure do."

"So do I. It's the bomb!" Though Kevin was old enough to be Lucas' dad, he couldn't believe how much they had in common.

"One mix coming right up." Lucas mixed them each a glass and returned to the living room. "Here you go," he said, handing a glass to Kevin.

"Thanks, Man."

As they were sipping their concoctions, the front door opened, and in walked Peggy Williams, Lucas's mom.

Kevin stood up, like a true gentleman. "Hi, Mrs. Williams. I hope you don't mind me coming over unannounced."

She looked surprised to see him. "No, it's not a problem, as long as you don't mind all these boxes."

"Here, Mom, let me take those," Lucas said, taking two shopping bags out of her arms, and carrying them into the kitchen.

"So, Mr. Myers, what brings you by?"

"I wanted to talk to you about the video shoot for Lucas' single before we go into production."

The phone rang before Kevin could start his spiel. Lucas answered. "Hey, man, what'z up? Hold on a sec." He put his hand over the phone. "If you don't need me, I'ma take this call in my bedroom."

"No, Lucas, go right ahead," Kevin said. Once Lucas had left, Kevin started up the conversation. "The reason why I'm here is to ask if Lucas can take a few days off of school and shoot his video? He told me that he's starting a new school, and I thought this would be the perfect time to shoot the video. That way he wouldn't have to miss any days once he started at Walburton."

Peggy looked skeptical. "I don't think that's such a good idea, Mr. Myers."

"Please, call me Kevin."

"Kevin, my late husband believed in education, as do I. And I don't want to send Lucas the wrong message by letting him skip school whenever he feels like it."

"Mrs. Williams…"

"You can call me Peggy."

"Okay, Peggy, this isn't a lame excuse for Lucas to stay out of school. This is work-related. His record and video need to be released at the same time, in order to maximize exposure. We're almost finished recording, and need to start on the video as soon as possible," he explained.

Peggy nodded her head, as if contemplating what he was saying.

As she sat there without saying a word, Kevin couldn't help but think how pretty she was. She had short black hair, a cappuccino complexion, was tall and slender, and had a striking resemblance to the actress Thandie Newton. Kevin didn't know how old she was, but she didn't look a day over thirty-five; especially in the jeans and tee shirt that she wore.

"I hear what you're saying, Kevin, but I've already scheduled Lucas' enrollment date."

"Since it is a private school, maybe you could call and

reschedule. Lucas is such a pro that the shoot shouldn't take any longer than a couple of days."

Hearing accolades about her son softened her resolve. "It's okay, if you're sure it won't take any longer than three days."

"I promise." Kevin stood to leave. "Thanks so much for your cooperation, Peggy. Trust me; I only want what's best for Lucas, just like you do." He smiled.

"I appreciate that, Kevin. Lucas really looks up to you. As you know, his dad died when Lucas was a baby, so he never knew his father. I'm so glad that he has a positive male role model in you," she said sincerely.

Kevin smiled. "Thanks, Peggy. That means a lot. I'll talk with you soon," he said and left.

Peggy walked back to Lucas' room and opened the door. "What do you want for dinner?"

"Hold on, man," Lucas told his friend Devin. "I don't care, Mom. Whatever you fix. I'll be off the phone in a few."

"Okay," she said and closed his door.

"Man, looks like we're going to start shooting my video soon," Lucas said. Even though he was on the phone, he had been standing by the bedroom door and had heard every word that Kevin and his mom had spoken. "Kevin came out tonight to ask my moms if I can take a few days off before starting Walburton."

"Word?"

"Yep, and she said yes."

"Where you gonna shoot at?"

"I don't know yet."

"Don't forget yo' boy. I wanna come down and watch all them video-hoes shaking their butts." Devin laughed.

"What makes you think I'ma have a bunch of hoes on the set? My joint is gonna be classy."

"Whatever, dude. Just make sure I get to meet some of the dancers. Them girls that be on them videos is tight!"

"You such a dawg, Devin. Don't you already have a girlfriend?"

"So. What's that's gotta do wit' anythang?"

"I thought having a girlfriend meant that you're committed to being with her," Lucas said, sounding like an old-fashioned guy.

"Whatever. I ain't married. Until I say 'I do,' I ain't gonna say, 'I don't' to the honeys. Besides, I'm just lookin', and what's the harm in dat? And speaking of lookin', when you start yo' new school, I wanna come over and check out them private school babes."

"Dang, man, what am I? Your personal pimp? You want me to set you up on the shoot, at school, what's next? You gonna have me making a video of you to post on YouTube?"

"Now that's not a bad idea."

"Ain't gonna happen. You my boy and all, but I swear sometimes we are as different as night and day. I want a steady girlfriend, and you want to screw around with as many chicks as you can."

"What can I say? I'm a ladies' man!"

"Devin, you too many things. Look, man, I gotta roll before moms comes back in here. Holla."

"Holla."

When Lucas hung up, he had to laugh. Devin was a character, but they were best friends since kindergarten, and though they were different in some respects, Devin was like the brother that Lucas never had. A horny toad of a brother, but a brother nonetheless.

5

"So, have you worked with her?" Reagan asked, pointing to a petite blonde.

Madison looked at the magazine. They were spending a lazy afternoon in Reagan's bedroom lying on the bed, flipping through fashion magazines. "Yeah, that's Uta Vongstuben. Everyone calls her UV. She's from Germany and is supposedly the next Kate Moss." Madison turned up her nose. "But if you ask me, she can't touch Kate."

"UV, that's ironic since she's as pale as a ghost and could use a few UV rays on that transparent-looking skin. Besides, she's not as pretty as Kate, and she's way too skinny."

Madison laughed. "If you think she looks skinny in that picture, you should see her in person. One strong wind could knock her to her knees, she's so thin."

"Madison, I don't know how you can stand working with all those non-eating, wafer-thin models. Doesn't it make you feel self-conscious?"

"No. The anorexic look is out. I may not be a triple zero, but I'm a healthy size four, and proud of it. Some days when I'm not bloated, I can even get into a two. Luckily I have a naturally high metabolism, and burn calories fast. I can eat anything I want and not pile on the pounds."

"I wish I could say the same. I have to watch everything that goes into my mouth. You know how much I love Cherry Garcia ice cream, but I can't have it every day, or my butt would be the size of a beach ball."

"Girl, you're being paranoid. What are you, a size six?"

"Yep."

"A six is still small. At least you're not a twelve."

"I'd wire my mouth shut before I'd get into double digits," she said, as if being bigger was a crime punishable by law.

"All this talk about food has me wanting a snack. What do you have to munch on?" Madison asked, rubbing her belly.

"I don't know. Let's go in the kitchen and see."

Reagan lived with her parents and twin sister Kennedy in a rambling five-bedroom co-op, but they were all out for the afternoon. "Let's see," she said, opening the refrigerator. "There's tuna salad, leftover meatloaf, mashed potatoes, cheese and crackers, fruit, and of course, ice cream."

"I think I'll have a meatloaf sandwich. Do you have any chips?"

Reagan took the meatloaf out, set it on the counter, and opened the cabinet next to the fridge. "There's plain, barbecue, and the baked, no-salt kind."

"I'll take the plain ones, as long as they're salted."

"Yeah, they have salt." Reagan fixed them each a sandwich, and poured two glasses of cranberry juice. The girls sat at the kitchen counter and munched away.

"So what was with you at Ian's?" Madison wanted to know.

"What do you mean?"

"I mean when Ian and I came out of his bedroom, you were acting all strange and stuff. Pulling on my blouse, and joking about my hair."

"I'm sorry. I was just jealous," she confessed.

"Jealous of what?"

"It's just that you guys seem to really be vibing on each other, and I want a boyfriend who likes me the way Ian likes you," Reagan confessed.

"What are you talking about? PG is crazy about you."

"It's not the same thing you have with Ian. I couldn't care less about PG. Don't get me wrong, he's nice and all, but he's not my type."

"You mean because he's so skinny?"

"Yeah that, and he acts so goofy sometimes," she said, popping a chip into her mouth.

"He wasn't acting goofy when he tried to kiss you after he gave you that necklace."

Reagan fingered the diamonds in the center of the Atlas. "I know. He caught me completely off guard."

"You should've let him kiss you. Maybe he's a good kisser. There's nothing like a boy who knows how to lip lock," Madison said in a dreamy voice.

"Can Ian kiss?"

"Ooh, yes he can, and his lips are so smooth," she said, closing her eyes as if reliving the moment.

"So, Miss Thang…is kissing all you did?"

"Well…" Madison opened her eyes, and turned her lip up in a smirk.

"Come on. Give up the goods."

Madison put her elbows on the counter, and rested her chin in her hands. "…he wanted to do more than kiss, and started feeling me up."

"You mean he put his hands in your panties?" Reagan interrupted.

"He tried to, but I stopped him. I told him that I wasn't ready for that yet."

"What did he say?"

"It's not what he said, it's what he did," she said, giving Reagan a serious look.

"What? What? What did he do?" Reagan asked excitedly, hardly able to keep calm.

"He took my hand and put it on his thing."

"Ugh. What did it feel like?" Reagan had smooched PG, but had never touched his privates, or any other boys' for that matter.

"I didn't actually feel it feel it. I mean, I felt it, but through his pants. It was long and hard."

"Whatcha mean 'hard'?"

"I mean, it felt like he had a banana in his pants."

"Ugh. I want a boyfriend, but I'm not ready to be feeling on some guy's banana."

"I know. It did feel strange."

"What felt strange?" asked a third voice.

They both swung around and faced the doorway. Kennedy was standing there looking exactly like her identical twin sister, Reagan, with big brown eyes on maple-brown skin. The only difference between the twins was their hair. While Reagan relaxed hers and wore it bone straight, Kennedy's was a fluff of freedom, naturally flowing all over her head.

"Hmm, nothing." Madison giggled, and covered her mouth as if unwanted words would come tumbling out.

Kennedy walked into the kitchen. "If I had to bet, I'd say you were talking about boys, or clothes, two of your favorite subjects," she said, rolling her eyes to the ceiling.

"Whatever we're talking about is none of your business. And speaking of clothes, don't you think it's time to retire that old army jacket? You've been wearing that beat-up-looking thing for months," Reagan said, insulting her sister.

"Unlike you and Madison, I couldn't care less about clothes. Do you know that there are kids starving in the world, and what you two spend on shoes and designer purses could host a child in a Third World country for years."

"Oh, here it comes. Kennedy's holier-than-thou speech. Don't you ever get tried of riding your high horse?" Reagan asked.

"I'm not riding a high horse. It's just that I care more about ending world hunger and saving the environment than spending all my time in the mall shopping for clothes that will go out of style in a few months. The money you all waste at those trendy boutiques could really be put to good use," she said, sounding more like a parent than a sibling. Kennedy opened the fridge, and took out a bottle of vitamin water.

"I swear, even though you guys look exactly alike, you couldn't be more different than if you were born from different parents," Madison commented.

"Sometimes I wish we were," Reagan whispered underneath her breath.

"I heard that," Kennedy said. "Anyway, I'll leave you two to your gossip. I've got better things to do," she added, and walked out with her water.

"Dang, do you two ever stop bickering?" Madison asked.

"It's not me. It's her. She always has to put down whatever I'm doing, saying, or wearing. I swear, sometimes I really do wish she wasn't my sister. It'd be a lot easier if she were more like you."

"We all can't be fabulous." Madison laughed, and swung her red hair, trying to lighten the mood.

"Ha, ha, very funny. Now that Cruella is home, why don't we go over to Serendipity? Suddenly I'm in the mood for a big fat sundae. Besides, I don't want her overhearing our conversation."

"Sounds good to me," Madison said.

The two friends abandoned their sandwiches, went

back into Reagan's room, grabbed their designer purses off of the bed, and headed out of the apartment. At least at the dessert parlor they could speak freely about boys, clothes and whatever else they wished, without being judged by Kennedy's lofty standards.

6

"Next stop, One-hundred and Thirty-fifth Street," the conductor's voice rang out over the subway's intercom system.

Kennedy stuffed her geometry book and notes back into her backpack, got up, maneuvered her way across the crowded subway car, and stood by the sliding doors, waiting for them to slide open. She was on her way to her volunteer job at Green Gardens, an environmental preservation group.

"Hey, Ken, wait up!"

Kennedy stopped on the steps leading out of the subway station, and turned around to see who had called her name. "Oh, hey, Roshonda."

"Girl, I keep telling you to call me Ro," she said, sucking her teeth as if she were aggravated.

"Sorry. I forgot," Kennedy said half-heartedly.

As they exited the subway, and were walking toward Green Gardens' main office, Roshonda started quizzing Kennedy. "Girl, why you come all the way uptown to volunteer? Don't you live in 'White World'?" Roshonda had wanted to know more about Kennedy ever since the day Kennedy started volunteering, but Roshonda rarely had the chance to speak to her alone since they were usually in a group with the other volunteers, so she took this opportunity to get to know Kennedy a little better.

"What?" Kennedy asked, as if she didn't hear the questions.

Roshonda sucked her teeth again. "I saaaiiidd," she prolonged the word, "why you leave 'White World' to come up here?"

"Whatcha mean 'White World'?" she asked, trying to sound like an around-the-way girl. Unlike her sister, Kennedy was embarrassed by her family's address. They lived on the West Side in a multimillion-dollar co-op, within walking distance of Lincoln Center and Central Park. Even though their bi-level home was big enough for a family of ten, only Kennedy, her sister, mom and dad lived there.

"You know, an area that has all the nice stuff, like Starbucks, The Gap, Barnes and Noble, Banana Republic, and…"

"Harlem has Starbucks," Kennedy said, cutting her off.

"Yeah, but where you live has more top-of-the-line stores, and some real cute boutiques."

"How do you know where I live?" she asked out of curiosity. Although she and Roshonda had been volunteering together for the past few months, Kennedy hadn't shared too much personal information. She didn't want the rest of the kids that volunteered to think that she was privileged, even though she was.

"I overheard you talking to Ms. Jones last week. I wasn't trying to be nosey, but her door was open, and when I walked past, I heard you talking about living on the West Side. I didn't know that many black people lived in that area; that's why I call it 'White World,'" she explained.

Kennedy did remember talking to the director of Green Gardens. They had seen each other at Fairway, one of the neighborhood markets, and were surprised to learn that they were neighbors. Suddenly, Kennedy felt embarrassed by her family's wealth, as if being prosperous was a sin. Most of the teens who volunteered at Green Gardens lived in Harlem. Kennedy wanted to fit in, and not be singled out because of her ZIP code. "The way Harlem is changing these days, it won't be long before you start calling it 'White World,'" she said defensively.

"Ump. You got that right. All these yuppies moving up here, 'cuz they can't afford 'White World' no more, make me sick. I remember a time when One-hundred and Twenty-fifth was full of street vendors, selling everything from beads to fake bags, to oils and incenses. Now they done made all them vendors move in a stanking lot, just so they can build million-dollar condos," she said, rolling her neck, and once again sucking her teeth.

Kennedy had successfully gotten Roshonda off of her back, and was glad, but before she could enjoy her victory, Ro started in again.

"What school you go to?"

Dang, here we go again. "Walburton," she said very softly, almost in a whisper.

"You mean Walburton Academy?" Roshonda said excitedly, nearly shouting. "They let you dress like that?" she asked, referring to Kennedy's tattered jeans, tee shirt and beat-up army jacket.

"No, we have to wear uniforms, but I always bring a change of clothes in my backpack."

"If I went there, I'd be so proud to wear my uniform and would probably rock it all day with a pair of fly shoes."

Kennedy was surprised to hear Roshonda say that. Ro looked like the poster-child for the radical-home-girl, with golden dreads tied up in a black-and-white mud-cloth-looking scarf, low-rider jeans, a tight black leather jacket and a huge Gucci bag with bamboo handles to complete her ensemble. Kennedy couldn't tell if the purse was a knock-off or not, but from the look of the plastic-looking handles, Kennedy assumed that it came straight from the counterfeits on Canal Street, instead of the Gucci boutique on Fifth Avenue.

"I hate wearing that stupid uniform. I'd rather wear my jeans any day."

"Why? You don't like going to Walburton?" Ro asked,

as if she couldn't fathom anyone not wanting to be a part of such a prestigious institution.

"It's okay," Kennedy said blandly, without any enthusiasm in her voice.

"Why you sound like that?"

"Like what?"

"Like it's a prison, and you gotta wear them orange state-issued jumpsuits. I love that school. I applied for a scholarship last year. My grades were good enough to get in, but I was turned down. Guess they had already filled their poor kid quota," she said, sounding broken-hearted.

Kennedy didn't know what to say. Not only did she go there, but so did her sister. Their parents wrote a huge check every year for not one, but *two* tuitions. "Oh," was all she said.

"Living in 'White World,' I'm sure your parents didn't have to rely on a scholarship to get you in." Ro turned to face Kennedy, as if a light had just gone off in her head. "Hey, what do your parents do anyway?"

Roshonda seemed bent on knowing more about Kennedy than Kennedy wanted to reveal. Kennedy realized that there was no use trying to pretend that she was from a lower income family, especially now that Roshonda knew that she lived in a pricy area of town, and went to a private school. "My mom is a make-up artist for Channel Seven, and my dad works for Time Warner," she said, trying to downplay her parents' success. In actuality, her mother was the key make-up artist for one of the soap operas, and her father was the chief financial officer for the mega conglomerate. "What do your parents do?" she asked, trying to get the attention off of herself and back on Roshonda.

"My dad is a train operator for the MTA, and my mom teaches nursery school. They make a decent living, but no way can they afford to send me to private school. That's why we applied early for this year's scholarship. Who knows, maybe I'll be in your class next semester."

"Yeah, maybe." Kennedy could imagine Reagan and Madison giving Roshonda the cold shoulder, and making fun of her fake designer purse.

Before Roshonda could get a chance to ask any more questions, they were at Green Gardens. They went right into the main room of the center, and waited along with the other volunteers for Ms. Jones to address the group. Five minutes after they had sat down, the director came into the room with an armload of pamphlets.

"Good afternoon, everyone." She smiled, and went right into her speech. "Nearly everywhere you look in Harlem, there's a construction crane. The vacant lots that we used to beautify with trees, plants and flowers are a thing of the past, being replaced by high-rise condominiums, and big-name businesses moving uptown. Since we're being forced out of the vacant lot business..." She chuckled at her lame joke and then continued, "I've come up with a brilliant idea. Well, it really isn't my idea, since they've been doing this in Europe for years now."

"Doing what?" Roshonda whispered to Kennedy.

Kennedy hunched her shoulders. "I don't know."

"Tommy, can you pass out these pamphlets?" she asked her assistant.

He went to each row of seats and handed a stack to the person seated at the end, asking them to pass them along.

"What the hell?" Roshonda said underneath her breath, as she looked at the cover.

"I know you're wondering what that is on the cover," Ms. Jones, said, as if she'd heard Ro. "It's called a Green Roof. This is a pitched roof that's been turned into a garden, with moss and sedum."

"What's sedum?" Kennedy asked aloud.

"Good question. They're a variety of plants with large, flat flower heads. They're very resilient, require little care, and can grow under almost any weather condition, which makes them perfect for roof gardens. If you look on page four, you'll see a manufacturing plant in Germany. On the left is the before picture of the roof. It's plain and barren like most roofs, but on the right, you'll see the after shot. No, it's not a picture of a park, but of the same roof."

The room suddenly filled with *oohs*, and *ahhs*, as the volunteers compared the before and after pictures.

"Wow, Ms. Jones, this roof looks like somebody's garden. It's beautiful," Kennedy said.

"I know. And not only is it aesthetically pleasing to the eye, Green Roofs are ecological as well as economical, by helping to absorb the sun and insulating the building during the winter months, and by absorbing rainwater to help eliminate flooding. Our first project is going to be the flat-top roof over on One-hundred and Twenty-fifth. The building is being gut-renovated, and we're going to transform the roof from an eyesore into a piece of living art!" she said enthusiastically.

"When do we start?" asked one of the volunteers.

"As soon as possible, but first I want us to take a walk over to the building to get an idea of the space, and also to get ideas from you guys on how we should design the garden. Come on; there's no time like the present," she said, ending the meeting.

Everyone gathered their belongings, and filed out. "Man, this is going to be some project. I never heard of a Green Roof before," Roshonda said, as they were walking down the street.

"Me neither. I can't wait to get started. I love plants. I'm always digging around in the garden when we're in Sag Harbor," Kennedy said.

"Your family has a house in the Hamptons?" Ro asked.

Damn! Kennedy hadn't meant to talk about their summer house; it slipped out. "Uh, yeah."

"What's this? The Parade of Stars?" a passerby asked.

"Ha, ha; not so funny," Ro said to her childhood friend, as he approached them.

"Where you guys marching off to?"

"This is my volunteer group, and we're going to check out our next project."

"Are you guys going to feed the feedless?" He laughed.

"I see you got jokes, Lucas, but they ain't funny," Ro said, with a straight face.

Kennedy stood there as the two talked. She didn't want to stare, but the boy standing in front of her was FINE! She didn't have a boyfriend, and wasn't really interested in anyone at her school; most of them were too pretentious for her tastes. But, this boy seemed cool, in his ripped jeans, and purple paisley shirt with the shirt tails hanging out. She wanted to be introduced, but didn't want to come off as a Desperado. *Say something. Don't just stand there like a mute. Say something clever!* she told herself; but nothing clever came to mind.

"Don't front, Ro, you know that was funny." He smiled, exposing a perfect set of chalk-white teeth.

"We better catch up to the group," Kennedy finally uttered. It wasn't clever, but at least she had opened her mouth.

Lucas looked at her, and they caught each other's eye, but neither said anything. Instead, he turned to Ro, and said, "Catch ya later," and then proceeded to walk away.

"Who was that?" Kennedy asked, once he was out of earshot.

"Oh, that was Lucas. We used to live in the same building, before my family moved on another block into a larger apartment. Anyway, I can't wait to get started on this new project," she said, changing the subject.

Kennedy wanted to find out more about Lucas, but she sensed that Roshonda wasn't about to give up the four-one-one on him, since she had quickly changed topics. *I wonder if he has a girlfriend?* Kennedy thought. As she listened to Roshonda drone on and on, her thoughts remained on Lucas, wondering whether or not she'd bump into him again, when she made her weekly trek to Harlem. Inside of her jacket pocket, she crossed her fingers, and prayed that she would see him again.

7

"Mr. Reinhardt, can I take your book bag?" asked Ian's chauffeur.

"Thanks, Bobby," he said, handing over his knapsack full of books, books that he had no intention of cracking. "And you can take PG's bag too," he said, as more of a statement than a question.

Bobby held the passenger door open with one hand, while he balanced the book bags with the other—never once complaining, as if it were his sole job to wait hand and foot on the spoiled-rotten, overprivileged brat *and* his friend. Once Bobby was back behind the wheel, he asked, "Are you going straight home, Mr. Reinhardt?"

"Yeah."

"So, how did you score the Benzo?" PG asked, once they were settled in the back of Ian's father's ultra-plush Mercedes Maybach.

"My parents are out of town."

"Where are they now?" PG asked.

"Utah."

"Utah? What the hell are they doing in Utah?"

"They flew there yesterday, to check out condos for Sundance."

"Sundance? The film festival isn't until January," PG said.

"I know, but they wanna get a jump on everybody to get the best crib."

"That sounds just like your parents to get the bomb place, so that they can trump all of their friends."

"Yep, that's them alright. They have to have not only the best, but the best of the best. Otherwise, they feel as if they're slumming."

PG ran his hand over the butter-soft, cream-colored leather seat. "This car is definitely, without a doubt, the best of the best. So, what's with it with them and film festivals? Weren't they in the Hamptons last week at a premiere or something?"

"Yeah," Ian said. "It's their new thing. Last year they were into major charity events, and this year, it's film festivals. They met that Redford dude at one of the charity balls, and now they're bosom buddies," he said mockingly.

The school was within walking distance of where Ian lived, and he could have easily walked the few short blocks home, but he liked flossing in front of his classmates. As they were chatting, Bobby was easing the long black Mercedes into the circular driveway of Ian's building. Bobby quickly jumped out, raced around to the trunk, opened it and retrieved their knapsacks. He then opened the passenger door with his free hand. The boys climbed out of the car, grabbed their bags, made their way inside of the building, and took the elevator up to Ian's penthouse.

Ian stuck his key in the door, but before he could turn it, Magdala swung the door open.

"Hola, Mister Ian." She smiled.

"Hey, Magdala. Whaz up?"

"Nothing up, Mister Ian. I take those," she said, holding out her arms for their book bags.

"Thanks, Magdala. Come on, PG, let's go into the den."

Once in the confines of the spacious, well-appointed entertainment room, Ian wasted no time making them drinks. "What's your poison?"

"A Goosing Bull."

Ian went behind the bar, mixed drinks for himself and his friend, and then joined PG on the sofa.

"So, Dude, back to your parents. Since they're into the movie biz now, if they need a pet project, I'm looking for investors for a screenplay I've been writing," PG said, guzzling his Grey Goose and Red Bull.

"A screenplay? When do you have time to write? Either you're at school or over here getting wasted."

"I know we're best friends, Ian, but, dude, you're not with me twenty-four-seven. For your information, after a few drinks, my imagination really gets to flowing, and by the time I get home, I got a nice buzz going; then I start writing. The days of being a cute little boy on a sitcom are long over, and I can't live off royalty checks for the rest of my life. That's why I've decided to try my hand at writing." PG stated his case, and then returned to the bar to freshen his drink.

"So, dude, what's your movie about?" Ian asked, polishing off his double vodka Martini. "And while you're up, fix me another one too."

"First, you gotta promise not to breathe a word to anyone. I don't want my idea getting out before I have a chance to shop it around."

"If I can't breathe a word about it, how am I supposed to tell my folks about it?" Ian smirked.

"Don't be funny. You know what I mean," PG said, suddenly sounding serious.

"Touchy, touchy. Lighten up, dude. I was kidding. Now tell me, what's it about?"

PG looked over his right shoulder, and then his left before speaking, as if Magdala was lurking around the corner eavesdropping. He then lowered his voice, and said, "It's about these rich-ass kids who go to a private school, and spend tons of money on the luxuries of life. They party like baby rock stars and don't have a care in the world."

"Wait a minute! That sounds like us!"

"I gotta get ideas from somewhere," PG said with a wicked grin.

"So you been taking notes on the stuff we do?"

"Not exactly."

"What the hell does that mean?" Ian asked, getting pissed.

"Why you getting all upset? It's not like I'm writing your life story."

Ian thought for a second. "Yeah, I guess you're right. But I'm warning you, PG, you better not put anything about me in your movie."

PG finished mixing their drinks, walked back to the sofa, and handed Ian his drink. "Why? Whatcha gotta hide, Ian?"

"I don't have anything to hide!" he said quickly.

"Are you sure?" PG raised his brow. "Sure you don't want to tell me about your private time with Madison? Like the other day when you guys went into your room. You had her back there long enough to get the panties." He looked at Ian dead-on, and Ian cast his eyes down to the floor. "Oh, that's it! You got the panties, and now you're trying to hide it!" PG said excitedly, as if he'd struck gold.

"For your information, we didn't do anything but kiss, but if we had, it isn't any of your damn business anyway," he said, leaving out the little detail of him trying to get Madison to give him a hand job. "And you better not make something up, and put it in your film," he said, knowing that PG had the tendency to make stuff up. Ian supposed it was a residual side effect from PG's days as an actor.

"Now would I do that?" he said slyly, before taking a sip of his concoction.

"I'm warning you. You'd better not," he said firmly.

Although Ian didn't want PG writing stuff about him and Madison, it wasn't their relationship that he was concerned about, but a secret that he didn't want revealed. He'd done a good job of keeping it hidden, and wasn't about to let anyone—including PG— discover what would certainly destroy not only his reputation, but life as he knew it!

8

"Dang, man, what did your moms pack in here?" Devin asked, as he struggled trying to get the oversized brown box through the revolving doors.

"Probably the kitchen sink." Lucas chuckled as he handled his own weighted box.

Today, Lucas and his mom, Peggy, were finally leaving the hood and moving to the Upper West Side, into a modest two-bedroom, two-bathroom condo.

"In a building as fly as this one, I'm sure the apartment comes with a sink," Devin shot back, as he made his way through the other side of the door, and surveyed the sand-colored marble lobby with its recessed lighting and colorful landscape paintings in exquisite gilded frames.

"Excuse me, young man, but where do you think you're going with that box?" the doorman asked, pointing at Devin.

"Yo, we going upstairs. My man Lucas here," he nodded his head in Lucas' direction, "just moved in," he said, and continued walking.

The doorman sprang from behind his marble command center, and blocked their path. "I don't think so!" He looked at them both as if they had landed from Jupiter.

Lucas and Devin both put their boxes on the marble floor, and then Lucas said, "It's true, my mom bought unit twenty-one D, and we're moving in today," he explained.

The doorman squinted his eyes at Lucas, as if doubting his claim. He then went back behind his desk, flipped through a notebook, and asked, "And what's your name? I need to check the move-in list."

"Lucas Williams, and my mom's name is Peggy Williams."

The overweight doorman ran his fat finger down the list of names, and stopped when he saw Lucas' and his mother's names. "Yes, you're on the list, but you're not allowed to move anything in or out of the front door," he said with a chastising tone.

"Why not?" Devin asked, before Lucas had a chance to respond.

"All moving and deliveries *must* go through the service entrance," he said, putting emphasis on the word, and pointing his chubby hand toward the rear of the lobby.

"And how were we to know that?" Lucas asked, with an edge to his tone, annoyed that this lard-eating-piece-of-flesh was talking to him like he didn't belong in this part of town.

"The movers know," was all he said.

Devin and Lucas had gone ahead of the moving truck, and had no clue where the service entrance was located. "Since the movers aren't here yet, can you tell us how to get to the back?" Lucas asked calmly. He realized that having an attitude with this dude was useless. Besides, he didn't want to get started off on the wrong foot. This was his new home, and for better or worse, he had to make the best of it.

"Go out the front, make a right, walk down about a quarter of a block, and you'll see the side entrance. There's a buzzer on the outside of the door; ring it and I'll let you in. Once inside, you'll see a bank of service elevators; use those to get to your floor. You got it?"

Lucas nodded his head yes, and then turned to Devin. "Come on, man," he said, picking up his box, with Devin following suit.

"Ole boy is guarding the place like it's Fort Knox or something," Devin said, once they were outside.

"Yeah, that's why I didn't want to move over here. These people are so snooty. Just imagine if the door-man has a 'tude, what the neighbors are like? I hate this bougie world," Lucas said as they made their way to the service entrance.

"I feel you, Bro. Why y'all move here anyway? What was wrong with your old crib?"

"My moms said that we had outgrown our old apart-ment. When we first moved in, I was a little kid, so she gave me the bedroom, and slept on the couch. She's been wanting to move forever, but we never had the money. Now with my advance, we could finally afford to move out. I told her I didn't want to move, and that I'd give up the bedroom and sleep on the couch, but she said no. She also said that this place is closer to my new school, and that I can walk instead of taking the subway."

"That's right! I almost forgot that you won't be going to PS-45 anymore. When are you starting Walburton?"

"After the shoot."

"When's the shoot gonna be?"

"Day after tomorrow. I can't wait; it's gonna be off da chain!"

"Don't forget you promised that I could come."

"I didn't promise nothing," Lucas teased.

"Don't trip, man," Devin said, with a serious expression on his face.

"I ain't tripping. It's just that Kevin said that it's a closed set."

"WHAT? Stop lying," Devin said, raising his voice.

Lucas busted out laughing. "Gotcha! Man, you should see your face. Look like you just lost your puppy. Calm down. I'm kidding. Of course you can come."

"See, man, you ain't right. You got my heart pounding and whatnot."

"Sorry, but after dealing with fatso at the desk, I needed a good laugh. The shoot starts at nine a.m., and will probably go all day and into the night, so you can come after school."

"Man, I ain't going to school that day. I'ma fake a cold, and once my peeps go to work, I'ma sneak out. I ain't about to miss all them honeys dropping it like it's hot."

"Speaking of honeys, I met this babe the other day. I didn't actually meet her…"

Devin cut him off. "What does that mean? Either you met her or you didn't."

"She was with Ro. We just gave each other the look. I didn't introduce myself, and neither did she."

"Aw, snap!! If she was with Ro, then she must be a chickenhead!"

"Why you say that? Ro ain't no chickenhead; she's pretty cool. I've known her since first grade. That's my girl, she's smart as hell, and volunteers in her spare time," Lucas said, coming to Roshonda's defense.

"Well, every time I see her, she's with that skank Trina. And you know that Trina be giving it up to anybody that asks. All you gotta do is look at her hard enough, and she's ready to drop them drawers." Devin laughed.

"Yeah, that may be true, but Ro don't sleep around. At least I ain't never heard no stories about her, and you know that if she was giving up the cooch, we'd know about it."

"True dat; true dat. Anyway, what about the honey she was with? What she look like?"

"Man, she was phine, with a 'p-h'! She has thick hair that she wears loose, and you know how I like that natural look. And she wasn't all dolled up like some of them chicks that be trying too hard. She was real low-key. She wore this old army jacket, rolled up at the cuffs. It was too big; probably was her dad's. Anyway, her eyes were big and brown, and her skin looked like maple syrup dripping off a short-stack," Lucas said in a dreamy-like voice.

"Dang, man, sounds like you digging her."

Lucas blushed. "I guess."

"Does she live uptown?"

"I don't know. I've never seen her before."

"Maybe she just moved into the neighborhood."

"Yeah, maybe."

"Why don't you call Ro, and get the four-one-one?" Devin asked.

"'Cuz I don't wanna seem like I'm lame. I can't be calling around asking about some chick that I don't even know," Lucas said, suddenly changing his head-over-heels tone back into an "I'm-da-Man" tone.

"True dat; true dat. Yeah, you don't wanna come off as desperate. Chicks don't like no wimpy desperate dudes. If she was with Ro, I'm sure you'll see her again."

"Yeah, man, I'm sure you're right."

As Lucas pressed the buzzer at the service entrance, he couldn't help but think about Ro's friend, and wonder when he would see her again. And next time, he planned on doing more than just looking.

9

"Peggy, this place is amazing," Norelle said, walking into the entryway of Peggy and Lucas's new condo.

Norelle was Peggy's friend from work. They were sales consultants at Barneys. What started off as two saleswomen working in the same designer department, eventually developed into a deep friendship. "Thanks, girl. I love it, too. I would've loved to have had a third bedroom to use as an office or guest room, but this is far better than that one-bedroom apartment that Lucas and I just came from. Come on in and let me show you around," Peggy said, shutting the door.

"I love these floor-to-ceiling windows. They allow so much light to come into the room."

"It's such a nice change from that dark apartment we lived in for years."

"Being in the back of a building has it advantages. It's quiet in the back, but dark like a cave."

"That's true. I love all this light. Being so high up I hope we don't get too much street noise. Come on, let me show you the kitchen." Peggy crossed the room, and led the way to the gourmet kitchen.

"Wow, Peggy, you have a Sub-Zero," she said, admiring the stainless steel, double-door refrigerator.

"Isn't it great? I never thought I'd have a designer refrigerator! That thing we had at the old apartment was two steps above an old-fashioned icebox. It wasn't self-defrosting, nor did it have an icemaker. And check out my new Viking range," she said, walking over to the stove.

"Wow! These stoves cost a fortune. I'm so happy for you, Peggy. You deserve all this and more," Norelle said, knowing how much her friend had sacrificed over the years, often working on her days off, for extra money.

Peggy looked down as if suddenly embarrassed by her fancy appliances. "Thanks. It's been a tough road. Ever since Lucas' dad died, I've been mother, father, and sole provider. Thank God Lucas landed a recording deal. Otherwise, we'd still be living pay check to paycheck."

"You did the best you could with what you had."

"Yeah, that's true. Come on, let me show you the bedrooms," she said, changing the subject.

They left the kitchen, and walked down a short hallway. There were doors on each side of the hall. Peggy stopped at the first door, and opened it. "This is Lucas' room. He hasn't gotten around to decorating it yet. There are still boxes everywhere, but it's twice as big as his old room, plus he has his own bathroom," she said, pointing to a door in the rear of the room. She shut the door. Peggy crossed the hallway, and opened the second door. "And here's my room," she said, stepping aside so that Norelle could enter.

"Wow!" Norelle said for the third time. "This room is so spacious. Even with your king-sized bed, you still have room for a dresser and loveseat."

"This room is big, isn't it? Plus, I have a private bath. I haven't finished decorating, but I finally have a real bed and don't have to sleep on the pullout any longer. This is one of those Tempur-Pedic beds that conform to your body shape. Come and sit down. You sink right in, but it's not too cushy."

"Nice," Norelle said, as her body sank into the custom-designed mattress. She then reached over to the nightstand, and picked up the picture frame that was sitting next to the lamp. "Who's this?" she asked, as she looked at the handsome face looking back at her. When Peggy didn't say anything, Norelle asked again. "Who's this? He sort of looks like Lucas."

Peggy stood there in silence. She hadn't expected Norelle to quiz her. She walked over, took the picture out of Norelle's hand, and put it back on the nightstand. "I've told few people about my past, because I didn't want their sympathy. But we've known each other long enough now, that I ought to tell you the whole story," she said, sitting down on the bed next to Norelle.

"What story?"

"The man in the picture is my husband."

"Your husband?" Norelle asked, a bit confused, since she knew that Peggy wasn't married.

"I should say my *late* husband, Marcus. Sometimes it feels like we were married yesterday, but then I come back to reality, and realize what we had is long gone." She sighed, and then continued. "Marcus and I were college sweethearts. Not only was he brilliant, but he was also an athlete. He was the point guard, and star of the school's basketball team. He was a first-draft pick for the Knicks, but wanted to graduate before entering the NBA. He believed in academia just as much as athletics. I guess that's why I'm so determined that Lucas gets the best education that money can buy."

"Yes, education is so important, but most young people think that material things come instantaneously, like in those videos. They don't realize that getting a college degree will, in turn, get you a good job. It's not like the old days, when a high school diploma carried you far. Besides, these days you practically need an MBA to really get paid. Don't get me wrong, I'm not saying that without a degree you can't make a good living, because there are some very successful people who have made millions without a college degree, but those cases are becoming few and far between," Norelle said.

"You're right. That's why, although I support Lucas' music career, I still want him to get an education. If he's going to be in the music business, he needs to know more than music. He needs to also know the business end of the industry, so he won't get screwed."

"That's true, I've read about so many artists who have been duped by their managers, and are now broke."

"Yep, that's why I'm stressing education. Anyway, before we graduated, I became pregnant, so Marcus and I decided to go down to City Hall and get married. We had planned on getting married anyway, but the pregnancy sped things up. We moved off campus into a tiny apartment. We were as poor as church mice, but as happy as two peas in a pod." She smiled fondly.

Norelle looked at her friend and could see the pain in her face. She reached out and touched her hand. "You're fortunate. Sounds like you guys had the real thing. Most people live their entire lives, and never find their soul mate."

"Yeah, Marcus was my soul mate, and I don't think I'll ever find that kind of love again."

"Don't say that. I'm sure there's another man out there for you."

"No, I'm done with love."

"Peggy, you're too young to give up on love."

"After what I've been through, I don't think I'll ever fall in love again."

"What could be so bad that you would say that?"

Peggy sighed hard. "The day I gave birth should have been the best day of my life. Seeing my baby for the first time brought such joy to my life, but that joy didn't last long…" She hesitated.

"What do you mean? Giving birth is such a special time."

"I know, but that wasn't the case for me. One minute, life was entering the world, and the next minute, life was being taken away," Peggy said, rather mysteriously.

Norelle didn't say anything; she sat there and waited patiently for Peggy to continue.

"I don't mean to sound mysterious," she said, looking at the confused expression on her friend's face. "The day Lucas was born was the day that Marcus died."

Norelle put her hand to her mouth and gasped. "Oh God, that's so tragic. How did he die?"

"He collapsed at practice. The autopsy later determined that he had a brain aneurism. Although I miss him terribly every day, the saddest part of it is that Marcus never got to see his baby boy. He was so looking forward to being a father. He would talk to my stomach all the time, telling his unborn son how much he loved him. And what's even sadder is that Lucas never got to know his dad."

"Wow, Peggy, that's some story."

"Yeah, a story with a sad ending," she said, with a tear forming in the corner of her eye. Peggy reached for a tissue from the box on the nightstand, and wiped her face. "Now you know why I'm through with love. Okay, let's change subjects, before I really start bawling. I don't like talking about that day. Even though it's been over fifteen years, it's still painful. Come on, let's go into the kitchen, and I'll make us some lunch on my gourmet stove," she said, eager for a diversion from the past.

As they walked back to the kitchen, Norelle's words, *You're too young to give up on love*, played in Peggy's ears, and she couldn't help but think that maybe her friend was right. Maybe one day she would find another soul mate. But that was a big "maybe." Finding another man like Marcus would be like ending the war in the Middle East—nearly impossible.

10

"Man, where the honies at?" Devin asked, looking around the empty set.

"Probably in the dressing room," Lucas said.

"This sho don't look like it do on TV. What's wit' all these cables and tape?" Devin asked, stepping over a pile of black wires as he entered the tent where Lucas was getting prepped.

"Those cables are for the cameras and lights," Lucas said as he sat in the stylist's chair, getting the final touches for his on-camera appearance.

The shoot was being held at an abandoned building in Harlem. Actually, it wasn't exactly abandoned, but was in the midst of being renovated. The crew had set up on the roof of the building for that ultra urban feel.

"Man, I thought this shoot was gonna be da bomb, wit' half-naked women running 'round shaking their rumps to the music like in a club; but this look just like some ole dilapidated, broke-down building like we see every day," Devin huffed, seemingly unimpressed.

"It's early yet. Wait until everything is in motion, and

then you gonna be singing a different tune." Kevin had told Lucas the rundown for the day, so he knew it was going to be long and drawn out.

"Man, I should have gone to school, and come by later," Devin said, parking himself in a canvas director's type chair.

"I told you to come by later, but nooo, you had to be here early."

"Yeah, yeah, whatever. At least I got to get my eat on at breakfast. Man, them waffles with strawberries and Canadian bacon was the bomb. They even had fresh-squeezed OJ. They always throw down like that?"

"I guess so. This is my first shoot, but I hear the caterers on these shoots don't play. They should be setting up lunch now."

"Man, all this free food was worth skipping school," Devin said, rubbing his belly.

"Is he about ready?" Kevin asked as he entered the tent.

"Yep, he's good to go," the makeup artist said, dusting Lucas's nose once more with a huge powder puff.

"Come on this way," Kevin said, the moment Lucas was done.

Half of the roof was underneath a huge white canvas that housed makeup, wardrobe, production equipment, and the catering area. The other half was where the video was going to actually be shot. "You're going to stand here," Kevin said, pointing to an "X" marked on the floor in red masking tape.

Lucas walked over to the "X," which was near the edge of the roof. "Right here?"

"Yep, that's good. The railing isn't that tall, so be careful not to fall over. I don't want to lose my star on the first take," Kevin mused.

Lucas looked down at the knee-high brick railing that circled the circumference of the building. "I'll be sure not to back up, 'cuz this little ledge definitely isn't going to stop me from tumbling over," he said, taking a few steps away from the edge.

"Now once the director yells 'action,' I want you to pantomime the words of the song. The record will be playing in the background, but you're not going to actually be singing. Got it?"

Lucas nodded his head. "Yeah, I got it."

"Good." Kevin turned to one of the production assistants. "You can go get the dancers now."

Within minutes, eight girls in micro-mini blue jean skirts, black midriff sequin tops, and black stilettos came strutting toward Lucas. Lucas looked over at Devin, who was practically drooling, and gave him a quick wink. Devin gave him a thumbs-up in return, as he ogled the dancers.

"Now I want you girls to dance around Lucas, and rotate so that he gets a chance to dance with each one of you. Understood?" Kevin said. Although he wasn't the director, he was producing the video, and he wanted to make sure that his ideas translated on tape. The girls all nodded their heads in agreement.

Kevin then stepped back out of the way, and went over to the director. "I think we're ready to start."

"Everybody in place. Cue music. Action!" yelled the director.

Instantly, the lyrics, *Turn around, baby, and let me hit dat thang, hit dat thang,* boomed out of the speakers and onto the set, while at the same time, a huge spotlight beamed in on Lucas. A fan began blowing on him causing his white shirt to fly open in the breeze, exposing his ripped abs, as he lip-synced. The dancers twirled around him, and he grinded up against the dancer who was directly in front of him when he mouthed, *Once I wrap my charms around ya, ya gonna be beggin' me to take dat thang, take dat thang.*

Devin stood with his mouth literally hanging open. He couldn't believe his eyes. It was like he was looking at a video on television, except this one was live. Lucas looked like a star as he danced on the rooftop, underneath the spotlight, with the city scene in the background.

"Cut!" yelled the director. "Makeup. Lucas and the girls need powdering. I'm getting too much shine from their faces."

When the makeup artist had finished retouching everyone, the director yelled "action" again, and again the action started. Kevin watched the monitor as Lucas fake sang, and bumped and grinded with the dancers like an old pro. His sexuality was oozing through the camera like someone twice his age. Kevin began smiling with pride as if he were watching his own son.

"Cut!" yelled the director once the song ended. "Let's take a break, have some lunch, and resume in an hour."

"How did I do?" Lucas asked, walking over to Kevin.

"Man, you were awesome. How'd you learn to dance like that?"

"Like what?"

"Like you've been making love your entire life. I mean you were moving your hips and grinding like you knew what you were doing."

"I taught him everything he knows." That was Devin putting in his two cents.

"Don't even front, Dev. I got my own moves. I guess it comes from watching them old videos of Marvin Gaye that my moms plays sometimes."

"Wherever it's coming from, don't lose it."

"Lose what?" asked Lucas's mom as she and Norelle approached the group.

Kevin turned around at the sound of the voice, and smiled when he saw Lucas' mom. "Oh, hi, Peggy."

"Hi, Kevin."

"Mom, what are you doing here?" Lucas asked, seemingly embarrassed. He was so glad that they were on a break. His mother would have probably freaked out if she had seen him bumping and grinding with the dancers.

"Norelle and I came over on our lunch hour. You didn't think I was going to have you tape your first video and not at least come over to see what you're doing, did you?"

"Mom, I'm not a baby, and don't need you spying on

me," Lucas said, sounding upset. One minute he was being praised for being a sex symbol, and now his mother was checking up on him like he was in nursery school.

"I'm not spying on you, Lucas. I wanted to come over to see for myself what it takes to shoot a video. You're making it sound like I'm not welcome."

"Of course you're welcome, Peggy," Kevin intervened.

"Come on, man, let's go back to my tent. I wanna check my cell to see if I have any messages," Lucas said to Devin.

"Have you two eaten yet?" Kevin asked the ladies once Lucas and his friend had left.

"No, we jumped in a taxi from the store and headed straight here."

"Come on. Let me show you the catering area," Kevin said, leading the way back inside the tent.

"You didn't tell me that this Kevin guy was fine," Norelle whispered, as Kevin walked ahead of them.

"I guess he looks alright," Peggy said matter-of-factly.

"He's more than alright. Look at that firm butt in those snug jeans, and I could live inside of those Yogi Bear brown eyes," Norelle said, sounding like a teenager with a crush on her teacher. "Is he single?"

"I don't know. I never asked."

"You should find out. He's a hottie."

"Frankly, I couldn't care less," Peggy said nonchalantly.

"If you're not interested in him, do you mind if I go for it?" she whispered.

"Norelle, I don't care what you do. It's a free country."

"You sure?"

"I don't have any claims on the man. If you're interested, don't let me stop you."

"Ladies, there's a nice selection of sandwiches, and over here we have a pasta station where you can pick a combination of sauces, and pastas. There's also a salad bar, with a variety of toppings," Kevin said, giving them the layout of the catering area.

"That sounds great, but what's for dessert?" Norelle asked suggestively.

"Good question. We have freshly-made ice cream sundaes, or if you're watching calories, we have frozen yogurt. But you ladies don't look like you have anything to worry about. Now if you'll excuse me, I need to set up for the next shot," he said, walking away.

"Now that's a fine man," Norelle reiterated once Kevin was gone.

Peggy shook her head. "You are one man-hungry woman."

"Girl, it's been months since my last date, and I'm long overdue."

"What happened to what's his name?"

"You mean Robert? He turned out to be a bore. All he wanted to do was rent documentaries, and stay in, so I had to let him go. I'm still a young woman, and I do like to go to the club and shake my groove thang," she said, getting a helping of mixed greens.

"Okay, Ms. Groove Thang, do your thang," Peggy joked, and then looked at her watch. "We'd better hurry up and eat, so we can get back to midtown before we're late," Peggy said, walking over to the pasta bar.

After finishing with lunch, the women went back to find Lucas. "Have you seen my son?" Peggy asked Kevin, who was talking to one of the lighting technicians.

"I think he's in his tent. It's back near the food area. Are you leaving?"

"Yes, we have to get back to work."

"Thanks for stopping by, and thanks for letting Lucas delay school for a few days," Kevin said warmly.

"You're welcome. See you later," Peggy said, and turned to leave.

"Good-bye, Kevin," Norelle said in a come-hither voice.

"See ya." He waved, and focused his attention back on what he was doing.

"Knock, knock," Peggy said, standing outside of the entrance to her son's tent.

"Hey, Mom, come on in," Lucas said, instantly recognizing his mother's voice.

Peggy and Norelle walked through the cloth doors. "My, my, this is very nice. You have your very own little living room. I love that love seat; is it suede?" she asked, walking over to the small sofa.

"I don't know," Lucas said.

Peggy ran her hand across the surface. "No, it's ultra-suede. Maybe we should think about getting one of those for your room. Instead of black, maybe a nice, rich brown. What do you think?"

"That sounds dope," Lucas said, as he sent a text on his cell.

"Okay, Son, we're going to get back to work now. I'll see you tonight. And come right home after the shoot, okay?"

"Yeah, Mom. See ya."

As soon as Peggy and Norelle left, Lucas was called back to the set.

"We're basically going to do the same thing, except this time I want you to sit on the ledge, and let the girls sit on your lap, one at a time. Got it?"

"Yep," was Lucas's response.

The director called for action, and once again the music began to blare. Lucas mouthed the words, while the spotlight beamed down on him; and the dancers each took turns dancing on his lap as if they were giving him a provocative lap dance. The shoot went on for hours, with Lucas changing positions a few times.

"Cut! Okay, guys, that's a wrap for the day. Good work," the director said.

"Lucas, you were awesome," Kevin said, walking over and slapping Lucas on the back. "Today went so smoothly that we should be able to wrap it up by tomorrow. Lucas, I called a car service to take you guys home. The driver should already be downstairs."

"Word?!"

"Don't sound so excited; it's not a stretch limo—just a Town Car."

"That's still cool. At least we ain't gotta get on the train. Okay, Kevin, see ya tomorrow."

Lucas and Devin excitedly bounced off the set and downstairs into the waiting car. "Man, that was off da chain! I mean, them babes were FINE, especially that Indian-looking chick. You think you can get her digits for me?" Devin asked, once they were settled in the backseat.

"Man, that chick ain't thinking about no high-schooler. She's probably in her twenties," Lucas said, dismissing Devin's request.

"Yo, I can get wit' da older babes as long as they fine, and like I said, she was all dat, and some cream."

"Whatever. Let me call my moms, and see if there's anything to eat at the crib. As much food as was at the shoot, I really didn't eat much. Guess I was too nervous about performing in front of the camera." Lucas reached inside his front jeans' pocket for his cell phone, but it wasn't there. "Man, have you seen my cellie?"

"The last time I saw it was when we were in your tent, and you were texting," Devin said.

"Excuse me, driver, can you turn around and go back? I left my phone at the shoot."

"Sure, no problem."

Ten minutes later, they were pulling up in front of the set. "I'll be right back," Lucas said, and hopped out of the car.

As he was running into the front entrance, someone was coming out, and they bumped smack dab into each other. "Uh, uh…" He was at a loss for words. Standing before him was the girl from the other day, the one who was with Roshonda. She was the last person he expected to see. Lucas had planned on really laying on the rap next time he saw her, but all he could say was "uh."

11

"Class, yesterday I told you to think about lab partners. In the past I've assigned lab partners myself, but the groups didn't work out as well as I had hoped, so this year I'm trying a new experiment. After all, this is a chemistry lab, so experimenting is what we do." Mrs. Vance chuckled, and then continued, "Remember, there are four people to a group, so if you've chosen your groups, will you please sit accordingly?"

Instantly, the class began to shuffle around, until nearly everyone was seated with their partners. Only a handful of students stood off to the side, and Kennedy was one of them. She looked around, and wasn't surprised to see her twin sister, Reagan; Madison, Ian, and PG huddled together at one of the lab benches near the back of the class. "Ump," she retorted at the sight of them.

"Now for the rest of you that are left standing, break off into groups of four, and take a seat."

"You wanna be partners?" asked Sid, one of the class geeks.

"Sure, why not?" Kennedy responded.

"What about you, Reese and Tony?" Sid asked two other students.

"Okay," they said in unison.

"Look at that motley crew," Madison said, cocking her head in the direction of Kennedy and her new lab partners.

"They look like they came from the Land of Misfit Toys. Kennedy, wearing that old tired army jacket over her uniform; Sid with his too-big eyeglasses slipping off his nose; Reese, with her oily, stringy hair looking like a life-sized Raggedy Ann doll; and Tony…" She stopped and pondered Tony for a second. "…well, Tony isn't all that bad. He has a killer bod, and cute dimples. Hey, why isn't he hanging out with us instead of the Misfits?" Reagan asked rhetorically.

"'Cuz he's a Brainiac, and couldn't care less about being cool or a jock," PG shot back, as if he were the King of Cool.

"He can study with me any day," Reagan said, dreamy-eyed.

PG jerked his head in Reagan's direction. "What does that mean? Are you saying you wanna get with him?"

"Chill out, PG. I'm simply saying that I wouldn't mind being Tony's study partner. Anyway, it's not like I'm your woman." She rolled her eyes, and landed them back on Tony.

"Class, open your textbooks to page one-hundred and three," Mrs. Vance said, then waited until everyone was on the same page.

The teacher was talking, but Kennedy didn't hear a word she said. She was too busy thinking about the day before.

"Can I help you, young lady?" the security guard had asked Kennedy.

Kennedy thought it was odd that a guard was at the entrance to a vacant building. "I'm from Green Gardens. We're planting an eco garden on the roof and I came by to get some ideas," she explained, and took a step forward.

He put his arm across the doorframe. "Sorry, you can't go up."

"Why not?"

He sucked his teeth, as if annoyed by her question. "They're shooting a video on the roof, and only authorized visitors are allowed inside."

"I promise, I won't be in the way. I want to go up and take a quick look around before our meeting tomorrow. I have a few ideas and want to make sure they're going to work," she said, trying to sway the beefy guard.

"No one's going up without a security pass," he said point blank.

"Oh." Kennedy had come all the way uptown, and hadn't expected to get turned away.

With no choice but to leave, she turned around, and ran straight into Roshonda's friend. They both stood there like two deer caught in a hunter's crosshairs. Kennedy was trying to think of his name, and all he could say was "Uh."

"Lucas, I was getting ready to hop in a car and head over to your place. You left your cell phone in the tent," some guy said, rushing out of the door.

That's right; his name is Lucas, Kennedy thought.

"Thanks, Kevin," Lucas said.

Kennedy watched the exchange, and felt as if she were in the way, so she turned and walked back to the train station.

"Now, class, there are two experiments on each page," the teacher said, interrupting Kennedy's walk down memory lane. "We're going to do both, and the two teams with the best results will win a spot in the science fair."

"You wanna do this one?" Tony asked his group as he pointed to the first experiment.

Kennedy hunched her shoulders. "I don't care." She wasn't interested in science experiments; all she cared about at the moment was getting to know Lucas. But as luck would have it, they had seen each other twice, and twice they had walked away without exchanging numbers, or names for that matter. *Oh well, such is life*, she thought, and then tuned her attention back to the project at hand.

12

"I don't think this thing," Renée Reynolds turned up her nose, "is appropriate for Madison to wear," she said to the stylist. They were on a photo shoot for *Teen Vogue*.

"I assure you all the teens are wearing halter dresses for summer," the stylist shot back in defense.

"I realize that, but this dress is, number one, see-through, and number two, there's barely enough material in the front to cover her breasts," Renée said, holding the dress up to the light, and scrutinizing it from front to back.

Trying to solve the dilemma, Madison said, "Nancy, let me try it on. It probably looks better off the hanger." Madison used the name that Renée insisted upon. Grandmother or Nana—and heaven forbid Granny—was too pedestrian for Renée Reynolds, the former runway queen and fashion icon.

"That's a good idea," the stylist agreed.

"Not going to happen. My granddaughter will not be wearing that thing, not even for one second," Renée shot back.

"Look, it's not like this is Madison's very own personal layout. She's modeling clothes like the rest of the other girls. So what's the big deal?" the stylist quizzed Renée.

Renée took a step closer to the stylist, lowered her voice in a menacing tone, and then said, "Obviously, you're new to the fashion world and have no idea who you're dealing with. Where's your boss?"

"Come on, Nancy, she didn't mean anything by it," Madison said, coming to the stylist's defense.

"Go sit down, dear, and let me deal with this. I'm not about to let them exploit you in this, this *thing*," Renée said, tossing the dress on a nearby chair, and then returning her attention back to the stylist.

"Does your grandmother always act like a vicious Rottweiler, ready to pounce if she feels that her 'Wittle Maddy Waddy' is being taken advantage of?" Reagan whispered, once Madison joined her on the sofa near the rear wall.

"Stop teasing. It's not funny. I'm almost seventeen, and the last thing I need is for my grandmother to speak for me. I'm perfectly able to talk for myself," Madison said, underneath her breath, as she watched her grandmother ream out the stylist in front of the art director.

"You can save your breath today, sweetie, 'cuz Ms. Nancy is giving that poor stylist a mouthful," Reagan said, as she watched Renée's mouth going a mile a minute.

Madison dropped her head for a second, and then said, "How embarrassing."

"Madison, come here, please!" Renée yelled across the room, once she was finished with her tirade.

Madison was humiliated, and felt like walking out the door. She was the only model at the shoot who had a chaperone—a bossy chaperone at that. Instead of walking out the door, she walked over to her grandmother. "Yes, Nancy?"

"You're going to be modeling these beautiful floral dresses," she said, handing Madison dresses that looked like they were more fitting for a ten-year-old hunting for Easter eggs, instead of a sophisticated teenager like herself.

"These?" Madison asked, scrunching up her face.

"Yes. The boat-neck covers up your breasts, and besides, the fifties look is back in. At least now you won't look like a call girl."

"No, just a little girl," Madison mumbled.

"What did you say, dear?"

"Nothing."

"Okay then, now hurry up and change. The photographer is all set and ready to go," Renée instructed as if she were running the shoot. And in a sense, she was. Having been in the business for eons, she was revered, and very few had the guts to cross her—at least those who knew better, which obviously the stylist did not.

Once Madison emerged from the dressing room with the cutesy dress on, the makeup artist tweaked her makeup, and then the hairstylist quickly wrapped her long auburn hair into a loose ponytail with tendrils hanging on the sides, before Madison stepped in front of the camera.

"Okay, give me a Hollywood red carpet pose," the photographer said.

Madison put her hand on her hip, and struck a haughty pose.

"That's great. Okay, now turn your head away from me, look over your right shoulder, and give me a pout."

Madison did as instructed while the photographer clicked away.

Two rolls of film later, Madison was back in the dressing room, changing into another stupid, adolescent-looking dress. The routine was the same as before. After two more changes, an hour later, the photo shoot was over.

"Great work!" the photographer told Madison.

"Thanks. It was fun!" she said, and walked toward her grandmother, who was beaming with pride.

"Dear, after you change, I want you and Reagan to go straight home. I would drop you off, but I'm running late for a dinner appointment." She reached into her purse, took out her Hermès wallet, and handed Madison two crisp twenty dollar bills. "Here, you girls take a taxi, instead of that dreadful subway."

Although Madison had her own money from working as a model, she took her grandmother's loot just the same. "Thanks, Nancy."

Madison did a quick change back into her Seven jeans,

graffiti tee-shirt, and Roberto Cavalli leather jacket. "I'm ready," she told Reagan once she reappeared from the dressing room.

The girls left the loft, went downstairs and hailed a taxi on West Broadway. "Sixty-first and Madison," she told the driver.

"That's not your address. Didn't your Granny tell you to go straight home," Reagan said, in a mocking tone.

"She did, but since she's not here to scrutinize my every move, I can do what I want. And I want...no, I NEED to go shopping. Wearing those kiddie-looking dresses made my skin crawl."

"Come on, Madison, it wasn't that bad. Those dresses were okay."

"Next time, you get in front of the camera and wear them," Madison shot back with attitude.

"I don't think so. I'll stick with getting my dresses from Barneys, thank you very much!"

As the girls were discussing their fashion preferences, the taxi driver was pulling up in front of Barneys, one of their favorite stores on Madison Avenue. Madison paid the driver with some of her grandmother's cash. The girls eagerly hopped out of the backseat, made their way through the front doors of the ultra-chic purveyor, and then made a beeline straight to the designer purses.

"Oh, I love this bag," Madison squealed.

"Is that the new Marc Jacobs?"

"Yep! I saw it in *Vogue* last week." Madison rubbed

the soft leather like she was petting a puppy. "I've got to get this," she said, bouncing to the checkout counter, without even glancing at the price tag.

"Will that be cash or charge?" the salesclerk asked.

Madison quickly handed over her AMEX. "You don't have to wrap it; I'm going to wear it."

"Sure thing," the clerk said. She rang up the pricey purse, took off the tag, and handed it to her customer.

Madison dumped the contents of her old purse into the new bag, and threw it over her shoulder. The saleswoman put her old purse in a shopping bag, and then gave it to her. Madison and Reagan twirled around on their designer heels, without saying thank you, and headed upstairs to where the clothes were located.

"Now this is a dress," Reagan said, taking a black mini dress off the rack.

"That's hot. I love the mesh at the top; it's such a great contrast to the solid body of the dress."

"Yep, and look at the back," Reagan said, flipping the dress over.

"Now that's what I'm talking about," Madison said, referring to the deep scoop of mesh going midway down the back. "Who's it by?"

Reagan looked at the label. "It's by Chloë Sevigny."

"Yeah, that's right. I read that she had started designing clothes now. It seems like nearly every star wants to get in the fashion game. P. Diddy really kicked it off; now movie stars are following suit," Madison commented.

"Hello, girls, can I help you?" asked the saleswoman.

"I want to try this on," Reagan said, nearly shoving the dress into the woman's arms.

"Okay, I'll start a fitting room for you. If you need anything else, my name is Peggy, and I'll be glad to help you." She smiled.

They both gave her a fake smile in return, without opening their mouths.

"I hate it when they call us 'girls,'" Madison said, once the woman had walked away.

"I know. We're nearly adults. Besides, I'll bet my clothing allowance is more than she," Reagan pointed her head in the saleswoman's direction, "makes in a week."

Madison pulled a Citizens of Humanity black denim jumper off the rack, and they walked toward the saleswoman, who was standing behind the counter. "I'll need a dressing room, too," she told the woman, and handed her the jumper.

"Sure thing," Peggy said, and led the way into the dressing room.

Ten minutes later, they came out, and walked back to the counter. "We'll take them. And ring them up separately," Reagan said curtly.

"Okay, do you want to apply for a Barneys card today?" Peggy offered.

"I already have one," Reagan said.

"Of course you do," Peggy said flippantly, getting fed up with their attitudes.

Reagan handed over the plastic. Once her transaction was over, Madison did the same. With their new purchases wrapped neatly in shopping bags, they bounced out of the store, as happy as they could be.

"I hate those bratty rich kids," Peggy said to Norelle once they had left.

"They have such a sense of entitlement. Did you see the new Marc Jacobs purse that the redhead had swinging off her shoulder?"

"Yeah, I saw it. That bag costs more than the rent at my old apartment. I tell you, those girls wouldn't know the value of a dollar if it reached up and slapped them in the face. I'm glad my son doesn't date spoiled girls like that," Peggy said.

"Well, with him going to that private school, don't be surprised if he brings a girl like that home to meet you."

"Bite your tongue, Norelle. Lucas is way too smart to get mixed up with a spoiled little brat, like those two."

Peggy hadn't thought about the possibly of her only son getting involved with a privileged rich girl. She had been focusing her attention on him getting a top-notch education. But, the more she thought about it, the more she realized that there was indeed a good chance that Lucas would start dating a privileged debutante. At that thought, she rolled her eyes, and then went off to help the next little rich brat.

13

The video shoot wrapped up in two days, thanks to Lucas's professionalism, and his ability to follow directions. Now was the moment that he had dreaded for weeks—his first day at the new school. All the paperwork and payments had been taken care of by his mother weeks ago, so Lucas begged her not to come with him on his first day. He didn't want to look lame, being escorted by his mother, like it was his first day of kindergarten. Peggy didn't like the idea of him walking in by himself, but she understood, and agreed.

Lucas walked through the huge wrought-iron gates of Walburton Academy, with his leather backpack swung over his left shoulder. He was nervous, but had that outward air of confidence. Lucas had never worn a uniform in his life, and felt awkward in the navy blazer with the gold crest on the left breast pocket, khaki pants, white shirt, and navy-and-gold-striped tie. He glanced around the courtyard, and saw himself mirrored in every boy on the grounds. They all looked like prep-school clones. The girls, on the other hand, were a different story. Although they also had on uniforms, they wore their skirts short, with socks pulled up over their knees. Instead of generic backpacks, they wore designer tote bags. And they all seemed to have on expensive-looking shoes—designer no doubt.

"Hey! Watch where you're going!"

Lucas stopped in his tracks. "Sorry, man."

Ian and Lucas stared each other down.

Who is this nerd, with the crease running down his pants? That crease is so sharp I bet if I touched it, I'd cut my finger, Lucas thought.

This dude obviously doesn't have a Magdala at home to iron his pants, Ian thought, taking in Lucas' rumpled uniform. Even his blazer was wrinkled. "You must be new," Ian said, looking Lucas up and down.

"You could say that," he said, not wanting to admit that he indeed was the new kid on the block.

"New or not, you're walking toward the teachers' entrance."

Lucas felt stupid, but didn't let it show. "Yeah, man, I knew that."

"Ian, who's your friend?" Madison asked, walking up.

"I'm not his friend," Lucas quickly replied.

"No truer words have ever been spoken," Ian said, looking down his nose at Lucas.

Madison also gave Lucas the once-over, and couldn't help but notice how rumpled his uniform was. "Did you enroll through the scholarship program?"

Lucas crinkled his face. "What?"

"Are you here on a scholarship?" she asked again, assuming by his appearance that he was from an under-privileged family.

"Naw, I ain't here on no damn scholarship! I'm paying my way, just like you," he spat out, obviously offended.

"Sorry. It's just that some of the urban kids are here on an academic scholarship, and I thought..."

Lucas cut her off. "Yeah, you thought that just 'cuz I'm Black, I'm from an *urban*," he said, mocking her word, "area, and couldn't possibly afford to be here without a handout."

Madison's cheeks flushed candy-apple red. "No, it has nothing to do with race. As a matter of fact, my best friend is Black, uh, African American," she stuttered, trying to redeem herself.

"Yeah, that's what they all say."

"Look, dude, she didn't mean anything by it," Ian said, coming to his girlfriend's defense.

"*Dude*, I really don't care what she meant," Lucas said, and strutted off, leaving them standing there looking stupid.

"What the hell is his problem?" Madison asked, once Lucas was on the other side of the courtyard.

"He's probably embarrassed to admit that he is indeed here on a scholarship. And when you called him out, he got mad."

Madison hunched her shoulders. "Yeah, I guess you're right."

"Right about what?" Reagan asked, as she joined them.

"See that dude over there in the wrinkled uniform." Ian nodded his head in Lucas's direction.

Reagan glanced around the school yard until she spotted the new guy. "You mean the hobosexual-looking dude? Looks like somebody shook him up in a bag, and then tossed him out?"

Madison giggled. "That's funny, where did you get hobosexual from?"

"Judging from the looks of him, he surely isn't meticulous about his looks like a metrosexual," she said, continuing to size him up. "He looks more like a hobo."

"When we were talking to him, and I asked if he was here on a scholarship, he got all defensive, and basically accused me of being a racist."

"What? That's ridiculous! Did you tell him that I'm Black?" Reagan asked.

"Yeah, that's when he said something smart and walked away," Ian said.

"He's probably mad because his parents couldn't afford to send him to Walburton without a scholarship. I mean, look at him." They all turned and stared in Lucas's direction. "He needs a haircut; those curls are all over the place. His uniform is too big, probably donated. If I had to bet, I'd say that he's one of those smart-ass kids from Harlem, Brooklyn, or the Bronx that scored high on his exams, and got offered a scholarship," Reagan said, making her own assessment.

"I'm sure you're right," Madison agreed.

"I mean he's cute and all, but unfortunately for him, I don't date broke dudes," Reagan stated, as she continued to stare at him.

Lucas had the feeling that he was being scrutinized underneath a microscope. Like all eyes were on him. He knew without a doubt that it was the redheaded chick, and Mr. Crease, so he turned in their direction. And sure enough, they were sizing him up like he was on display, but another girl had joined their little huddle. He squinted his eyes for a clearer view, and couldn't believe who was standing there with them. It was the girl he had bumped into at the shoot—Roshonda's friend. Except she looked different. Her hair wasn't wild like before, but straightened, and she didn't have on her old army jacket. *Damn, I thought that chick was cool, only to find out that she goes to this uppity school, with these rich brats. So much for trying to get with her,* Lucas thought and shook his head. Just then, the bell sounded, and he walked through the doors of Walburton Academy along with the rest of the "rich brats."

14

"So, man, how was the first day?" Devin asked.

Lucas was sitting at his computer, checking email. "It was a'ight."

"Just a'ight? C'mon, tell me somethin'. What was da honies like? Did any of them step to you?"

"Man, them chicks got they heads too far up their butts to notice anybody," Lucas said, as he clicked away on the keyboard.

"Don't tell me didn't nobody give you no rhythm? Don't they know who you are?" Devin said, as he sat on Lucas's bed, and fiddled with the controls on his iPod.

"Yeah, they know who I am, a'ight. They think I'm a welfare reject."

Devin looked up from the tiny gadget in his hands. "Whatcha mean?"

"Man, there was this tall redheaded chick who asked if I was there on a scholarship," Lucas said, as he wheeled around to face his friend.

"What? You mean she straight up asked if you was poor?"

"Basically."

"Damnnnn, man, that's cold. Why you think she asked you that?"

"'Cuz I wasn't dressed like them, and wit' da paint job I got," he said, pointing to his skin, "I guess I don't look like no preppy dude from the East Side."

"Wait a minute. I thought you had to wear a uniform."

"I do."

"Whatcha mean you wasn't dressed like them?" Devin was curious.

"First off, I had my moms order my uniform a size too big, 'cuz I didn't want it fitting just right, like some nerd. And then I slept in it, so that it'd be all wrinkled, and stuff. I wasn't about to stroll up in there looking all bright and shiny like some new penny fresh out the mint."

"Word!" Devin slapped Lucas a high-five. "I bet you looked like some heathen hood rat." Devin laughed.

"Yep!"

"But tell me this…when she asked if you were there on a scholarship, why didn't you tell her the truth?"

"'Cuz I didn't want them phony fake wannabes liking me 'cuz I'm a singer. If they don't like me for who I am then…," he put up his middle finger, "…'em."

"I heard that. But what's going to happen once your single and video drop? They gonna be all over you then."

"Yeah, I know. But once my joint drops, I'll know who my real friends are, and them rich brats at Walburton ain't on the list."

Devin held up his hand and again slapped Lucas five. "I'm sho glad I'm on the list." He grinned.

"Oh, oh," Lucas said, raising his voice, "Man, I forgot to tell you who I saw in the school's courtyard as I was waiting for the bell to ring!"

"Who?"

"Roshonda's friend!"

"You mean that chick you saw with Ro uptown?"

"Yep, the one and only. Man, I thought she was from around the way, but she's one of them. She's a snob," Lucas said, with disdain oozing from his voice.

"Just 'cuz she goes to a private school doesn't mean she's a snob."

"Yeah, I know that, but you didn't see the way her and her friends were staring me down, like I had crawled up out the sewer. That's why I didn't want to go to that school, 'cuz you gotta look and act a certain way to be accepted."

"Man, once yo' joint drops, Ro's friend is gonna be singing a different tune. She gonna wanna be getting wit' a brother." Devin grinned some more.

"She can forget it. Even though she's fine, I don't wanna be dealing with nobody who likes me 'cuz I'ma rapper. Kevin told me about girls like that, and I can't be bothered," he said, turning his attention back to the computer.

"Word!" Devin agreed, and began fiddling with his iPod again.

Kennedy was at home, underneath the covers, nursing a cold. Her bed was littered with tissues that she had used and discarded. She had her chemistry book open, but wasn't really in the mood to study. Instead, she was watching an afternoon talk show, and today's topic was teen pregnancy. The last thing Kennedy had to worry about was getting pregnant, unless it was an immaculate conception like in the Bible. She didn't have a boyfriend, so the chances of knocking boots were nil, and even if she had someone special, she still wouldn't be sexing him up. She wasn't ready for all of that yet. Since she wasn't planning on being a teen mother, she switched channels. As she was channel surfing, the telephone rang. She was the only one in the house, so she picked up.

"Hello?"

"Hey, Ken. What's up?"

"Uh…nothing. Who's this?" she asked, not recognizing the voice.

"It's me, Ro."

"Roshonda?"

"Girl, how many times do I have to tell you to call me Ro?" she said, annoyed that Kennedy kept forgetting her nickname.

"Sorry. So, Ro, how did you get my number?"

"I got it from the emergency list at the center. I figured since you didn't come to the meeting today, something must be wrong, 'cuz you never miss a meeting, so I decided to call."

"Oh."

"What's wrong?"

"I have a cold. I didn't go to school, and didn't feel like trekking uptown. I've been in bed all day," she said, grabbing a tissue and blowing her nose.

"Oh. I hope you feel better. We went over to the building today, and started laying out the design for the roof garden."

Kennedy let out a sneeze. "Excuse me."

"Sounds like you could use some rest, so I'ma let you go. I just wanted to make sure you were alright."

"Thanks. See you later." Kennedy was about to hang up, but she decided not to. "HEY, RO!" she yelled into the receiver, before Roshonda disconnected the line.

"Yeah, what's up?"

"Uh..." Now that she had Roshonda's attention, she didn't quite know how to broach the subject, so she just spat it out. "I ran into your friend the other day."

"What friend? I got lots of friends."

"That boy we saw when we were on our way to visit the vacant building for the first time."

"You mean Lucas?"

"Yeah, Lucas."

"Where'd you see him?"

"I went back to the building to get some ideas, and we bumped into each other in front of the building. So... how do you know him?"

"We go way back. Why you asking? You like him or

something?" Roshonda asked, getting right to the point.

Kennedy started to blush, and was glad that this conversation was taking place over the phone. "No, I don't like him. I was just curious, that's all," she lied.

"Um-hmm." Roshonda was wise beyond her teenage years, and knew a crush when she heard one. "I bet."

"I'm serious!" Kennedy said quickly. "I was only asking."

"Okay, 'only asking.' Anyway, Lucas is my boy, so the next time we see him, I'll introduce you. Since you so curious and thangs." She chuckled.

"Don't bother. Anyway, it's not like I'm looking for a boyfriend," she said, trying to hide her true feelings.

"It ain't no bother. I gotta go; my moms is calling me. Later," she said, and hung up.

Kennedy continued to click through the television channels, but her mind was on Lucas, wondering when she would see him again. And this time, they were sure to have a conversation, especially with Roshonda making the introduction. Kennedy couldn't help but smile at the thought. Lucas was fine, and exactly her type.

15

Ian was locked away in his room. His parents were absent as usual, and as usual he took advantage of the time alone. He had planned a small get-together, but before his friends arrived, he had some work to do. He sat in front of his iMac, and clicked away on the keyboard. Ian was so engrossed in what he was doing, that he barely heard his cell phone ringing until the fourth ring. He reached for it while still focusing his attention on the screen.

"Hello?"

"Dude, where are you?" PG asked.

"I'm at home," Ian answered in a far-away, distracted tone.

"We're downstairs, and the doorman has been calling up for the past five minutes. Dude, you sound strange. What the hell are you doing?"

"Uh…I was just on the computer. Tell the doorman to call the house phone again, and I'll pick up." Ian could hear PG in the background talking to the doorman, and a few seconds later, the cordless phone rang. "Hello… yes, send them up." Ian pressed the end button, threw the phone back on the bed, and dashed into his closet. He threw on a Tom Ford, black button-down, and kept on his jeans. He then went into the bathroom, and ran his fingers through his hair for that controlled, tousled look. Before leaving his bedroom, Ian logged off the computer, turned off all his electronics, and shut the door.

He walked into the living room—which was dark now—and switched on the dimmer to the track lighting, creating a romantic effect. He then walked over to the stereo system, and just as he turned on the CD player, his friends were ringing the doorbell.

"There you are. We were beginning to think that you stood us up," Madison said, kissing Ian on the lips.

He grabbed her tiny waist, and pulled her to him. "Now why would I want to stand up the most beautiful girl in Manhattan?"

Reagan cleared her throat at his comment.

"Sorry, Reagan, didn't mean to leave you out of that statement. I meant to say the most beautiful *girls*, plural." He smiled, then added, "And, you ladies are looking quite yummy this evening."

"Thanks, sweetie. We were at Barneys the other day, and made a few spendy purchases. You like my new bag?" she asked, showing him her Marc Jacobs.

"Love it. Love it," he gushed, sounding like a gay fashionista.

PG rolled his eyes at their silly exchange. "So, Ian,

what had you so preoccupied that you didn't hear the phone?" he asked, eagerly changing the subject and walking into the living room.

"Oh, nothing much. I was just on the computer, that's all. You know what a time warp the internet can be." He took hold of Madison's hand, and led her into the living room. "What can I get you guys to drink?"

"The usual for me," PG said.

"I'm in the mood for a pomegranate martini. Do you have any of that Pomm juice? It's the bomb! Not only do you get a buzz from the vodka, but at the same time you get a glass full of anti-oxidants. Did you know that pomegranate juice is supposed to be one of the healthiest juices out there?" Reagan asked.

"Yeah, I heard that. Ian, make that two pomegranate martinis. I might as well get in on the craze," Madison said.

"But of course, my love." He kissed Madison on the cheek. "I'll be right back," he said, and disappeared into the kitchen.

A few minutes later, Ian resurfaced, with not only the pomegranate juice, but a tray of hors d'oeuvres. "If anyone's hungry, I have some munchies," he said, and set the silver tray on the cocktail table.

Reagan walked over and picked up a Swedish meatball on a decorative toothpick. "Hmm, these are tasty."

PG walked up to Reagan, and ran his hand up her arm. "Not as tasty as you, I'm sure."

Reagan rolled her eyes, polished off the meatball, and reached for another.

"So…," PG looked around the room, "are we here alone?"

"Yep," Ian said, standing behind the bar, mixing drinks.

"Where's Magdala?" Madison asked.

"At home."

"Isn't she supposed to stay overnight when your parents are away?" Reagan quizzed.

"Yes, she is, but I told her I was spending the night over at a friend's, and insisted that she go home."

"Aren't you the clever one?" Madison said.

Ian took a mock bow. "Yes, that would be me. Now get over here, and pay for this drink."

Madison walked behind the bar, threw her arms around his neck, and planted a big, wet, juicy kiss on his mouth. "Does that cover my tab?"

He patted her on the butt. "It'll do for starters."

As Reagan watched them, a twinge of *frienvy* washed over her. She loved her friends dearly, but couldn't help but envy the relationship that they shared. They seemed to be so in love, and couldn't keep their hands off of each other. She, too, wanted a boy who was a knockout, not skinny, bumpy-faced PG. Suddenly, her mind flashed back to the new guy in the school yard. He was extremely fine. Even through his scruffy appearance, Reagan could see that he was gorgeous. His skin was the color of a penny. It looked as if he had a permanent tan, and even though his curls were unruly, they were shiny and black. He was tall, and didn't appear to be skinny, but she couldn't tell for certain since his uniform was covering his body. If only he wasn't poor, she'd make a move on him. But she wasn't about to give up PG, with his extravagant gifts, for some no-name scrub, who probably couldn't even afford to take her to Mickie D's for a Happy Meal.

"So, PG, you wanna dance?" Reagan asked, peering over at Madison and Ian, who were engaged in a battle of the tongues.

PG nearly wasted his drink, as he put it back on the bar. "Sure," he said, and rushed over to Reagan. He immediately pulled her close to him, even though the song playing was a fast cut.

Since I haven't found Mr. Right yet, Mr. Right Now will have to do, Reagan thought, wrapping her arms around PG's shoulders, and shutting her eyes, pretending that he was the "One."

16

"I'll have a venti decaf with a double shot of hazel-nut, and a chocolate croissant," Kennedy told the barista. She and Roshonda were at the Starbucks on the corner of One-hundred and Twenty-fifth Street, having coffee before the Green Gardens meeting started.

"And I'll have a venti Caramel Macchiato, and a blue-berry muffin," Roshonda added. She took her wallet out of her purse, reached inside and took out a twenty. "I got it," she said, handing the cashier the money.

"Ro, you don't have to pay for me. I have money."

"I'm sure you do, Ms. West Side, but it's my treat. Consider it a get-well gift."

"I'm not sick anymore. It was just a slight cold. Really, Ro, I can pay," she insisted.

"Look, Ken, just say thank you. And if it makes you feel any better, you can treat me next time," Roshonda said, taking her change from the cashier.

Kennedy blushed. She wasn't used to girls being nice to her. Most of the chicks at Walburton were so selfish that the thought of treating a friend to a coffee was probably not even in their realm of thinking. Even her own sister had never bought her anything—except for grief and ridicule. "Thanks, Ro. I really appreciate it."

"No problem," Ro said, walking over to the pick-up counter with Kennedy following behind.

Once they had their drinks and munchies in hand, they found a table by the window and sat down.

"So what did you guys go over at the last meeting?" Kennedy asked.

Roshonda pulled out a drawing from her oversized purse, and unfolded it. "This is a diagram that I drew of the roof. Over here," she pointed to an area on the paper, "is where the flower beds will be."

"Wow, you really draw good; this diagram looks like it was done by a professional," Kennedy commented, peering over at the drawing.

"Thanks. I wanna be an architect, and design buildings all over the world, like that dude who did the addition to the Louvre."

"With the way you draw, I'm sure you'll be a great architect."

"Thanks, girl."

"So, what's going to be over there?" Kennedy asked, referring to a blank spot.

"We haven't decided what's going to go in that corner yet. I guess we'll figure it out this afternoon, when we walk over to the building."

"Oh, good, at least I have a chance to add my two cents." Kennedy chuckled.

"Two cents is better than no cents." Ro laughed.

As they were laughing at their lame jokes, Roshonda looked out of the window, and spotted two friends of hers. She tapped on the glass to get their attention. "Come here," she mouthed, and crooked her finger.

Kennedy watched her movements, and couldn't believe that Ro had invited that boy Lucas and another guy to join them. Suddenly, she felt self-conscious about her appearance. Normally she didn't care that her hair was all over the place like a hippie, or that her old army jacket looked like it was ready to be donated to Goodwill, but with the gargantuan crush she had on Lucas, all of that had changed. For the first time in her life, Kennedy wished that she was polished like her sister. She didn't even have any lip gloss in her bag; the only thing she had remotely resembling a beauty product was a half-used tube of Vaseline. Kennedy smoothed her hand over her unruly hair (wishing now that she had a perm). She quickly took off the army jacket, stuffed it in her knapsack, and pulled down the front of her T-shirt, trying to straighten out the wrinkles. Just as she finished adjusting herself, they approached the table.

"Yo, Ro, whatup?" Lucas asked.

"Yeah, Ro, what's poppin'?" Devin asked, eyeing Kennedy up and down.

"Nothing much. Just sitting here wit' my girl, going over the plans for this rooftop renovation Green Gardens is working on."

Lucas didn't say anything, just nodded his head, and cut his eyes at Kennedy.

"Lucas, I want you to meet my girl…"

He cut her off, "Yeah, I know who she is."

Kennedy looked up at him (for the first time), surprised that he knew who she was. *Maybe he remembers me from the other day*, she thought.

Roshonda looked surprised, too. "Really? How you two know each other?"

"She go to Walburton," he said dryly, cutting his eyes at Kennedy.

Kennedy was shocked to hear that he knew what school she went to. *He must have asked Ro about me.*

"So, Ro, what's been going on?" Lucas asked, turning his attention to Roshonda.

"Nothing much, just the same ole, same ole; what's been happening with you? I been hearing some good stuff around the hood." She smiled.

Lucas shifted his weight from one foot to the next, and then stuffed his hands in the front pockets of his jeans, seeming discomfited by her question. He wanted to tell Ro all about his video shoot, and new CD, but he didn't want to discuss anything in front of the Walburton brat. He didn't want her running back and telling her friends his business. He wanted to be liked on his own merit, not because he was a budding star. "Yeah, it's all good," he simply said.

"Man, why don't you tell them about the…"

Lucas had the feeling that Devin was about to mention

the video shoot, so he cut him off. "Come on, man, let's bounce."

"Awe, man, we just got here. Let's stay awhile and kick it wit' da ladies," Devin said, still eyeing Kennedy.

"Yeah, why don't you sit down? We have some time to kill before our meeting starts," Roshonda said.

"I can't. I got some stuff to do for my moms," Lucas lied. He didn't feel comfortable around the new girl, and preferred to leave. Besides, he had a photo shoot later.

"Come on, man, let's at least get something to drink," Devin said, trying to encourage him to stay.

"Naw, I gotta go, but you stay if you want to," Lucas said to Devin. He then turned to Ro, and said, "See you around," purposely ignoring Kennedy.

"Yeah, see ya."

Once Lucas had left, Ro turned to Devin, who had parked himself in the chair next to Kennedy. "What's his trip?"

"I dunno." He hunched his shoulders.

"I wanted to hook him up with my girl here."

"Since Lucas ain't here, hook me up," Devin said, as if Kennedy wasn't even sitting there.

"Kennedy don't wanna be hooked up wit' no scrub. Lucas is more her speed," Roshonda said, point blank.

He rolled his eyes at Roshonda. "Whatever. So yo' name is Kennedy, huh?"

"Yeah, and what's yours?" Kennedy asked out of politeness, even though she could not care less.

"Devin, but the ladies call me…" he stopped for a

second, "…wait a minute, you must be that chick Lucas saw with Ro last week."

"Yeah, that's me." She smiled shyly.

"Aw, snap!"

"Why you say that?" Ro asked.

"Nothin.'" He blushed.

"Don't 'nothin' me, Devin. What you know? Tell me," Ro quizzed.

He looked over his shoulder, making sure no one was within earshot. "It ain't nothing really." He turned to Kennedy. "It's just that Lucas saw you at school the other day," he said, leaving out the fact that Lucas thought she was stuck-up.

"He goes to Walburton?" Kennedy asked, shocked. She had never seen him there before.

"Yeah, he just started the other day."

Kennedy thought for a second, and remembered that she had missed a day of school. *I bet he saw Reagan and thought it was me.* She started to tell Devin and Ro that she had a twin sister, but decided not to. Most people assumed that twins were inseparable, but she and Reagan were complete opposites, and she didn't feel like explaining their unsavory history. "Oh really?"

"He didn't want to go there but his moms insisted," Devin added.

Kennedy began to heat up inside; with her and Lucas attending the same school, she had a chance to get to know him. But just as soon as her blood began to boil, it instantly cooled down. *If he saw Reagan, I'm sure he's going to want to date her instead of me. She's probably just the kind of girl he's into—the fashionista type. Who would want to date me, looking like a boy in my baggy clothes and a washed-out army jacket?*

"Yo, Ken, that's great news! Since you and Lucas both go to Walburton, you guys can hook up," Roshonda said, full of excitement.

"I doubt that very seriously."

"Why you say that?" Ro asked. "I thought you liked him."

"It's a long story," she said, picking up her croissant and taking a bite. Kennedy was glad that it was Saturday; at least now she'd have the weekend to formulate a plan to get Lucas' attention Monday at school.

17

"**Y**ou and PG were pretty cozy the other night," Madison said into her cell phone. She had just finished a photo shoot and luckily for her, her grandmother had to leave to run an errand, but was picking her up in a few minutes.

"After looking at you and Ian grinding and giving tongue, you could say I sort of got in a quasi-romantic mood, especially with the martinis," Reagan responded.

"Yeah, those martinis were good. So good, in fact, they had me thinking about letting Ian pop the proverbial cherry," she whispered.

"WHAT?!" Reagan shrieked into the phone. "Are you serious?"

"As that new Maybach, and we both know how serious that car is. Anyway, I'm tired of listening to these models talking about how they got laid, and how good it was. They make it seem like having sex is the most wonderful thing in the world, and I'm beginning to wonder what I'm missing."

"Wow! That's a huge leap from feeling on his 'banana' to actually doing the deed."

"Yeah, I know, but the other night when we were dancing, his thing got hard again, and the more he pressed it into me, the more I liked it. It was like something inside of me woke up."

"That was your libido. I've read stories in *Cosmo* about that, talking about a woman's sex drive and stuff," Reagan said.

"I need to read that article, and find out more about this libido business. I mean I've heard of it before, but I've never experienced what I felt the other night. In a way, it sort of scared me," Madison confessed.

"What do you mean?"

"I mean, all the other times that Ian has tried stuff, I always wanted him to stop. But when we were dancing so close like that, I wanted him to keep going."

"Are you really ready for sex though?"

"I think so. There're so many girls in our class that have already had at least two lovers. Besides, Ian and I have been going out for forever, and I don't think he's going to wait much longer. He's always so horny, and has been trying to get into my thongs for a while now."

"Whatever you do, use protection. You don't want to be another teenage statistic, with a baby, or even worse, some kind of dreaded disease," Reagan said wisely.

"Oh, for sure. You can believe I'll be armed with a variety of condoms. I'm not going to rely on Ian to bring 'em. You know how irresponsible guys can be. As a matter of fact, why don't you and I go over to Duane

Reade, and see what's on the market? I never really shopped and compared before."

"Me neither," Reagan admitted. "Actually, that's a good idea. I think I'll buy some, too, just to keep in my purse. The idea of walking around with condoms sounds so..."

"Grown!" Madison added.

"Yeah, it does."

"Hold on; my other line is beeping." Madison switched over, and a few seconds later switched back to Reagan. "That was Nancy; she's downstairs." Madison picked up her bag and walked over to the elevator. "I'm getting ready to get in the elevator, so if I lose you, I'll call you back."

"Okay."

The elevator doors opened, and out came a group of people, and one of them bumped into her with a huge duffle bag. "Watch where you're going!" Madison huffed.

"Oh, excuse me, I didn't mean..."

"Hey..." She stopped and looked at him up and down, "aren't you that new guy I met at school the other day?"

Damn! It's that redhead from Walburton, Lucas thought.

"Yeah," he said, and hurried away before she had a chance to quiz him.

Madison stood there for a second, and stared as Lucas went into the photographer's loft that she had just come out of. "Rea, you won't believe who almost knocked me down."

"Who?"

"That new guy from school."

"You mean the one with the curly hair, and wrinkled clothes."

"Yep."

"What's he doing at a photo shoot?" Reagan wondered.

"He was carrying a huge canvas bag. I bet he's a part-time messenger; probably delivering film for the photographer," she said, stepping into the elevator.

"Yeah, I bet you're right. He probably has to work on the weekend to help pay for his books."

"What did you say? I'm losing you," Madison shouted into the tiny receiver, as she rode down to the first floor.

"Hello? Hello? I guess I lost her," Reagan said, and hung up.

Lucas couldn't believe his luck. Out of all the people he could've run into, it would be that nosey chick from school. He stepped off so fast that he didn't give her a chance to insult him this time.

"Right on time," Kevin said, walking up to Lucas and slapping him on the back.

"That's one of the things my moms drills into me on a regular basis. She hates being late, and says that getting to work on time is half the job."

"You mother is a wise lady. How is she doing?" Kevin asked, with a smile.

"She's fine."

"Good. Okay, today we're going to shoot the cover for the CD. Did you bring a change of sneakers, and shoes like I told you?"

"Yep. Got 'em right here in the duffle," he said, holding up the bag.

"Good. The stylist already has a change of clothes laid out for you for different looks."

"What about the pictures we took a few months ago? I thought they were for the cover."

"They were, but you've grown some in the last six months, and I want to update your photos," Kevin explained.

"Isn't it too late to be taking pictures for the album? I thought it would be dropping soon."

"It would be too late if we weren't living in the digital age. These pictures we take today, once we approve them, will be sent directly to the art department, and designed into the cover. Anyway, your single is dropping first. We're going to create a buzz before the CD drops, so we have time."

"Oh, I see," Lucas said, nodding his head.

"I looked at the final edit for the video, and it's ready for release. We just need to tweak the background vocals on the single, and then we're ready to rock and roll." Kevin grinned.

"When do you expect it to hit the air?"

"In the next week or so."

"Wow, that soon?"

"Yep. Aren't you excited?"

"Yeah, but it's gonna seem strange listening to myself on the radio."

"You'll get used to it. I've also lined up an interview on BET," Kevin said excitedly.

"Word!"

"Yep. I wanted to tell you the good news in person. I sent over your press kit awhile ago. They love your music, and are excited about having you on the show."

"Man, that's huge. Thank you. Once my moms finds out I'm gonna be on TV, she's gonna freak." Lucas smiled.

"I bet she's so proud of you."

"Yeah, she is. She says she wants me to go to college and get a degree, but I know that she's happy about my singing career, too."

"I'm sure. You just wait, Lucas. You're going to be a big star, and I'm not just blowing smoke," Kevin said, with a serious expression on his face. "Come on, let's get started with the shoot."

As Lucas followed behind, he couldn't help but think. *Just wait 'til that redhead and her clique see me on TV; then they'll know I ain't no scrub waiting for a handout!*

18

When the Green Gardens meeting ended, Kennedy said good-bye to Roshonda and rushed to the subway station. All during the meeting her mind was preoccupied. Instead of focusing on mulch, flowers and trying to save the environment, she was focused on shopping (a rarity for her). After seeing Lucas, and feeling like a slob, she decided to get a new pair of shoes to go with her uniform to try and spruce it up. The old army boots that she usually wore (to accompany the jacket), were way too bulky. She started to invite Ro to join her, but didn't want to make a big deal out of it, especially since Lucas had ignored her at Starbucks.

The train was approaching the station as soon as she reached the platform. Once the doors opened and some passengers got off, Kennedy boarded and took the train straight to the Village. She didn't know much about trendy boutiques—that was Madison and Reagan's area of expertise—but she did know that Eighth Street was where some really cool shoe stores were located.

She slowed her gait as she made her way down the

street, looking in the huge plate-glass windows of the various boutiques, at the different styled shoes. Some were spiked heels, some were platforms, and some were flats, all in varying colors from hot pink, to fire-engine red, to Big Bird yellow, and of course, most New Yorkers' color of choice—black. Kennedy spotted a pair of midnight-blue heels—the exact blue as the color in her uniform—with a brass square buckle, stopped, and went inside the store.

"See something you like, little lady?" asked the salesman.

"Yeah, the blue shoes with the buckle, in the window."

"Sure. What size?"

"An eight."

"Have a seat. I'll bring 'em right out."

Kennedy cleared a few shoeboxes off a chair and sat down. She looked around the store, and couldn't remember the last time that she was in a boutique. Their parents gave her and Reagan a monthly clothing allowance, but Kennedy always put the majority of hers in the bank. Unlike Reagan who spent every single dime.

"Here you go," the salesman said, flipping open the box and handing her the right shoe. "I also brought out a few other pairs of blue shoes, just in case you don't like that one."

"Do you have a footie?" Kennedy asked, pulling off her army boots and sweat socks.

"Sure," he said, handing her a box of nylon footies.

Kennedy slipped on the mini stocking, before putting

her foot in the shoe. She then rolled up her jeans, and walked over to the floor-length mirror. She turned to the left, and then to the right. She couldn't decide if she liked the shoe or not. Kennedy had worn sneakers or combat boots for so long that real shoes looked, and felt, funny. "How do they look?"

"Beautiful. Simply beautiful!" he said, spoken like a true salesman.

"Uhh… I don't know." She hesitated in the mirror for a few seconds, trying to envision the shoes with her uniform. Most of the girls at school wore their designer shoes with their knee socks pulled above their knees. She tried to imagine that slutty look, but it just wasn't her. Wearing "real" shoes was as far as she was willing to go—at least for now.

"Why don't you try them both on to get the real look," he suggested.

She limped back over to the chair, sat down and put on the other shoe. Kennedy went back over to the mirror, and studied her feet. The shoes did look good, and they were comfortable, something she wasn't expecting. "Okay, I'll take them."

"Great. Will that be cash or charge?"

"Do you take debit cards?" she asked, taking off the shoes, and putting them back in the box.

"Sure do. Come over to the register and I'll ring you up," he said, swooping up the shoebox.

He walked behind the counter, punched a few keys on the register, then said, "That'll be two-sixty-seven fifty."

"What?" Kennedy asked, assuming that she had heard him wrong.

"That'll be two-hundred, sixty-seven dollars, and fifty cents," he said slowly, as if she were hearing impaired.

Kennedy nearly choked. She had no intention of spending nearly three-hundred dollars on *one* pair of shoes. "Uh…I don't think I want them anymore."

"Why not? What's wrong? They looked great on you."

"Uh…they're a little too expensive."

"Expensive? Are you kidding me? Do you know how much these would cost in Barneys?"

She hunched her shoulders.

"If you don't know, I'll tell you…twice as much! That's how much!" he said, raising his voice as if offended.

"Oh," was all she said.

"As a matter of fact, these are on sale today. So don't come running back here, when you go to Barneys and find out that I'm telling you the truth," he said, with an obvious attitude.

Kennedy knew that her sister and Madison shopped at that expensive boutique store, and didn't think that he was trying to snow her. She thought about it for a few seconds. She had more than enough cash in her account to cover the purchase. Besides, she wanted to look good on Monday, *and* it wasn't like she splurged on a daily basis. "Okay, I'll take 'em," she said, handing over her debit card.

"Good. I promise you won't be sorry." He rang up

her shoes, and put them in a shopping bag. "Thanks for coming in, and have a good weekend."

"Thanks," she said, underneath her breath, still uneasy about spending so much money on shoes.

Kennedy took the train home, but before going straight in, she decided to stop by Duane Reade. She walked through the doors of the drug store, and went straight to the aisle for hair care products, looking for a relaxer to tame her mane. There were so many different types, from mild to extra strength, from lye to no-lye. It was all so confusing for Kennedy, so she decided not to put anything in her hair except a really good conditioner. She liked Lucas, but loved her hair more, too much to damage it with harsh chemicals. Next she went down the aisle filled with makeup. Kennedy had always gone au natural, and didn't have a clue what to buy. She didn't want to look like she was trying too hard with a face full of *paint*, so she decided to go with a lip gloss called "Nearly Nude." It was almost the shade of her own lips, but had a tiny bit of sparkle to give it some kick. *Maybe I'll get some mascara*, she thought. She perused the different brands of mascara, but there were too many to choose from—extra length, super extra length, super duper extra length…and so on. *Oh, forget it.* Exasperated, she went to the checkout aisle. As she was waiting in line for her turn, she spotted her sister and Madison up ahead. They had their backs to her, and didn't see that she was behind them.

"No, turn your card the other way," Kennedy heard the cashier tell Reagan.

"Look, I turned it the other way, and it still didn't work. Your machine must be broken or something," her sister huffed.

Kennedy shook her head at her sister's tone. *She can be such a bitch*, she thought.

"I'll just pay cash," Reagan said, stuffed her card back in her wallet, and handed over a twenty.

Kennedy watched the cashier put Reagan's purchase in the plastic bag, and nearly gasped when she saw what her sister was buying—CONDOMS! Kennedy wanted to rush up to her sister and ask whether or not she was having sex, but decided not to. Reagan would probably brush her off anyway, so Kennedy stood back and waited to see what Madison was buying. *Ohmigod, she's buying condoms, too!* Kennedy was shocked. She knew that Reagan and Madison were into boys, but she didn't know that they were into having sex! She wanted to run home and squeal to her parents, but decided not to. Besides, for all she knew, they were buying them "just in case," and not actually doing the nasty. In either case, it really was none of her business. Kennedy watched the two of them leave the store with their "contraband."

I'm gonna have to keep my ears, and eyes, open to see exactly what these two are up to! she thought, as she paid for her lip gloss.

19

Ian hadn't seen his friends since their little soirée; that night had been a blast. They drank martinis and nearly got totally wasted. He was feeding Madison one drink after the other in the hopes that she'd give him some. His plan almost worked, but she wasn't drunk enough to go back to his room. However, she did let him grind up against her, and feel her up. Normally she would back away the moment his hardness pressed against her groin, but that night she seemed to like it. Ian was perpetually horny. He wanted some sex badly, and didn't know how long he could wait for Madison to get ready. Thinking about getting down and dirty with his girlfriend was making Ian hot, and he knew just what to do for some quick relief. Everything in his room was set up perfectly, and he wasted no time getting down to business.

As Ian was in the midst of it, his celly rang. At first he ignored the call and let it go to voice mail, but no sooner had it stopped ringing than it started all over again. The phone was breaking his concentration, so he clicked a few keys on his keyboard, snatched the phone off his desk, and looked at the caller ID.

"Yo, dude, why are you calling me repeatedly like you don't have anything better to do?" he said to PG, annoyed.

"Geesh, what's gotten into you?"

"Nothing. I was busy, that's all. So, what's up?" Ian asked, ready to end the conversation and get back to his computer.

"Just finished adding a few more scenes to my screen-play."

"I hope you didn't take any creative license, and steal bits and pieces from the other night."

"Oh, you mean like when you had Madison pressed against the bar," PG said, with a smile in his voice.

"If you weren't so busy looking at us, maybe you could've gotten a little action of your own," Ian shot back.

"Oh...that's low. If you weren't so busy trying to grind a hole into Madison, you would've seen that I *was* getting some action of my own."

"You mean the charity dance that Reagan gave you?" Ian said sarcastically.

"Dude, it wasn't charity! She's really into me."

"Yeah, right. Keep dreaming. She's only into the gifts you keep giving her."

"Why don't we have another get-together tonight, and I'll show you how much she's into me," PG suggested.

"I wish I could, but believe it or not, my parents are home," Ian said, sounding disgusted.

"Dude, they're gone so much that I almost forgot that they lived there. Did you get a chance to tell them about my screenplay?"

"No. I've been in my room practically all day. I've been bummed out that they're in town this weekend. I was going to invite Madison over for a 'sleepover.'"

"Don't forget to tell them about my new project. They might be interested. So, you think she would have gone for that?" PG asked.

"Don't hold your breath. My parents are only into high-profile stuff, and your little screenplay won't shine the spotlight on them like they're used to. Anyway, I think Madison will be game. At least I hope so. Dude, I don't know how much longer I can hold out," Ian said, sounding exasperated.

"What's the problem? I thought you were seeing Reese on the sly?"

"I was, and, dude, when I tell you that she knows how to work that body of hers," he whistled, "I'm not kidding."

"Wow, who would think that stringy-haired Reese was a Freak of the Week. So, why you'd stop screwing around with her?"

"She wanted me to quit going out with Madison. Reese said that since she was the one giving it up, then she ought to be my full-time girlfriend, and not just a booty call," Ian explained.

"So, obviously you chose beauty over booty." PG laughed.

"Dude, it's not funny. There's no way I'd leave Madison,

who is a professional model, for a, a," he stammered, trying to find the right word.

"A life-sized Raggedy Ann doll," PG said, finishing Ian's sentence. "Isn't that what Reagan called her in class?"

"Yeah, she did. Reese isn't polished by far, but I do miss the way she polished the old helmet." Ian chuckled.

"So now that your booty call is history, when are you and Madison going to do the deed?"

"The next time my parents go out of town, I'm going to invite her over for the night."

"You think she'll stay all night?"

"I'm banking on it. I'm going to tell her to say that she's spending the night at Reagan's; that way she won't have to worry about coming in late."

"Sounds like you have it all planned out. Hey, why don't Reagan and I come along, and sleep in the guest room," PG said, devising a "Get-Laid" plan of his own.

"I don't think so, dude. It'll be Madison's first time, and I want to make it special."

"Yeah, it'll be her first time, but your what? Twenty-first?" PG joked.

"Ha, ha."

"So, does Madison still think you're a virgin?"

"She never asked me point blank, so I never had to lie."

"How convenient."

"Look, dude, I can't help it if she thinks we're both saving ourselves for each other."

"Poor disillusioned Madison. If she only knew her boy-friend was about as pure as the sludge in the Hudson River."

"What can I say? I'm a teenager with raging hormones," Ian said matter-of-factly.

"Rage on, dude. I'ma get back to writing. See ya in school Monday," PG said, and hung up.

Since he was homebound on a Saturday night, and was far from sleepy, Ian opened the mini-fridge—that looked like a nightstand—next to his bed, then took out two miniature bottles of vodka, and a can of Red Bull. He took a long swig from the can, nearly draining it, and then poured the vodka in. With his drink in hand, he turned his attention back to his computer, and finished what he had been doing before PG called.

20

Most people anticipated the start of the weekend, but Kennedy couldn't wait for Monday to come. Sunday night, she had ironed her uniform blouse. Normally, she wore it underneath her army jacket full of wrinkles. She then laid out the pleated skirt and monogrammed sweater on the extra bed in her room, along with a pair of navy knee socks. Next, she took her new shoes out of the box, and placed them at the foot of the bed. Kennedy stood back, surveyed her outfit and smiled. Though it was the same uniform that she had worn countless times, somehow it seemed different. It wasn't the uniform that was different, but her attitude. Gone was her "school is for learning" attitude; it was replaced by, "school is for getting to know Lucas' mindset." Unlike most teens who used school as a social network, Kennedy had always been focused on the books, until now. Now she was focused on Lucas.

Sleep eluded Kennedy Sunday night. She tossed and turned as if it were Christmas Eve, and tomorrow was the big day. The day when she would unwrap her long-awaited present. Exactly at five-thirty a.m., her eyes popped wide open. Normally, she awoke at six-thirty, jogged around the neighborhood, showered, dressed and made her way to school. This morning she was so full of nervous energy that she bounced out of bed, and instead of jogging a mile, she ran two. Kennedy used the extra hour to style her hair. After blowing it dry, she stood in front of the bathroom mirror and stared at her image. She didn't have a clue what to do next—shampooing, conditioning and blow-drying was as far as she went with her hair. Kennedy could hear Reagan's shower running, so she snuck into her sister's room, nabbed one of the many magazines off the nightstand, and went back in her own bathroom. Kennedy flipped through the pages, until she found a few hairstyles that she liked.

"Looks like I'm gonna need a flatiron for this look," she said to herself.

Kennedy didn't have a flatiron, but Reagan did, so she waited until she heard her sister finish showering to go back in her room. Kennedy tipped into Reagan's bathroom, and saw a flatiron lying on the sink, plugged into the wall. Obviously, Reagan was letting it warm up. *I better not take that one.* Kennedy opened a few drawers, hoping to find another iron.

"Bingo," she whispered as she opened the last drawer and found another flatiron. Kennedy went back into her bathroom, and began tackling her thick hair.

With her hair done, Kennedy went back into her

bedroom and took her time dressing, then gingerly added lip gloss to her lips. Instead of her old backpack, she went into her closet and took out the Tory Burch leather satchel that her godmother had given her for her birthday. She had never worn it before, but it went with her new look, so she dumped the contents of her ratty knapsack into the new bag—along with the lip gloss—and headed out the door.

Usually, Kennedy arrived at school early enough to get a spot near the wall by the entrance before the courtyard got full, so that she didn't have to deal with parading in front of the student body. She hated the judgmental eyes. But today, even though she had awakened an hour earlier, Kennedy had taken too much time getting ready. Now the courtyard was brimming with gossip mongers. She held her breath, and walked through the gates.

PG, Ian, Madison and Reagan were in their normal spot in the center of the courtyard, where they could see, and more importantly, be seen.

"So, how was your weekend?" PG asked Reagan.

"It was okay. I really didn't do too much," she said, leaving out the little trip that she and Madison had taken to the drug store to buy condoms. "What about yours?"

"It was good. Stayed around the house mostly," he said, preferring not to tell her and Madison about his screenplay. PG didn't want them trying to dictate what he should or shouldn't put in his movie, like Ian was trying to do.

"And what about you, Ian? What did you do?" Reagan asked.

Ian surely wasn't about to tell them about his internet escapade. That was one piece of information that was indeed private, and he planned on keeping it that way. "Oh, nothing much. My parents were home all weekend, so I basically stayed in my room, to avoid them."

The entire group seemed to be hiding secrets from each other. Some were big whoppers, and some were nothing to swat at, but they were secrets nonetheless.

"Omigod!" Madison shrieked.

"What?" the others asked in unison.

"Look at Kennedy," Madison said, nodding her head in Kennedy's direction.

Reagan's mouth dropped opened. She had been so busy quizzing her friends about the weekend, that she hadn't noticed her sister walk into the schoolyard.

"Wow," PG said, turning his head from Kennedy to Reagan. "I can hardly tell you two apart now."

"I know. With Kennedy's hair straightened like that, you two are identical," Madison added.

"Not quite," Reagan said, finally coming out of her momentary case of shock. "I still have a certain style that she'll never have—EVER!"

"I don't know about that. Look at that Tory Burch bag, and her shoes. Didn't we just see those in Barneys last week?" Madison asked.

"She didn't buy that bag. Our godmother gave it to

her," Reagan explained as if it canceled out the designer purse. "And those shoes are probably knockoffs. I can't imagine Kennedy shopping at Barneys. She's too cheap," Reagan huffed.

"Cheap or not, she sure looks good. She even ditched her old army jacket," PG added.

"Yeah, she sure does," Ian said, adding his two cents.

"Now, now. Down, boys. It's still just Kennedy, so don't go drooling all over yourselves," Madison said.

"Yeah, why would you want a fake Canal Street replica when you have the original right here," Reagan said, flipping her hair to one side.

"Wow, I still can't believe the change. What do you think inspired her?" Madison wondered aloud.

"Who knows? Better yet, who cares!" Reagan said, turning her back, preferring not to look at her sister any longer. Suddenly, it was like looking in a mirror, and she couldn't take the reflection.

As they were contemplating what made Kennedy alter her appearance, the bell rang, and they all filed into the school.

Kennedy was so glad that the bell had finally rung. She could feel Reagan and her cronies sizing her up when she walked into the courtyard. And sure enough, when Kennedy had glanced over at them, they were talking and glaring right at her. Reagan looked pissed—no doubt afraid of the new competition—while the others looked stunned. Kennedy could not care less what they thought. She wanted Lucas to get a look at the new her, but she hadn't seen him anywhere in the courtyard.

Normally, Kennedy enjoyed her classes, especially English, but today they were a serious snore. She kept hoping that Lucas would be in one of her classes, but so far she hadn't seen him. Kennedy couldn't concentrate on what her teachers were teaching, and felt like a zombie on auto-pilot, drifting from one class to the next. She dreaded going to her chemistry class, since she hadn't done her part of the homework assignment. Over the weekend, Kennedy was supposed to have written the theory of her group's experiment, but she was too busy thinking about beauty to think about science.

"Where's the hypothesis?" Sid, the geek of the group, asked the moment Kennedy sat down at their lab bench.

"Uh…uh…I left it at home," she lied.

"It's due today," he said, with his too-big glasses sliding down the bridge of his nose.

"Stop tripping, Sid. I'll hand it in tomorrow," Kennedy reassured him. She looked around the table. "Tony's not here anyway. So we'll both turn ours in tomorrow."

"Oh, didn't you hear?" Reese asked. "That's right. You were out on Friday."

"Hear what?"

"Tony transferred," Sid answered.

"What a shame. He sure was a stud," Reese commented underneath her breath.

"What you'd say?" Sid asked.

"Oh nothing," Reese said. She then swiveled around on her stool, glanced around the room until she spotted Ian and his *girlfriend*. She gave him a dirty look, rolled her eyes, and then turned back to her group.

"Now that we're missing a person, maybe Mrs. Vance will give us more time to complete the experiment," Kennedy said.

"But we're not…" Before Sid could finish his sentence, up walked their new lab partner.

"What up?" Lucas nodded, sitting on the stool left vacant by Tony.

Kennedy couldn't believe her eyes. There he was in the flesh, looking better than he had the last time she saw him.

"What are you doing sitting at this bench? Shouldn't you be over there with *your* crew?" Lucas asked Kennedy.

"Uh…uh… I'm at the right table," she answered nervously.

Lucas turned around in the direction of Ian's table, getting ready to make his case, but quickly snapped his neck back to Kennedy. He looked across the room directly at Reagan, then back at Kennedy. If he didn't know any better he would have sworn that he was seeing double. But what he was seeing were twins. "Uh… uh…" Now it was his turn to stammer. "You've got a twin!" he said, as more of a statement than a question.

"Yeah, but don't hold it against me." Kennedy chuckled.

Lucas looked back at Reagan, as if studying her. "Okay,

okay, I can see a slight difference. Her hair is straighter, and," he turned back to Kennedy for comparison, "she has on more makeup."

"There's more than hair and makeup that defines our differences."

"Like what?" he asked, looking directly into Kennedy's eyes for the first time since that day he saw her on the street with Ro.

"For starters, she's a snob, and I'm not."

Lucas thought for a second. "Oh snap! That was her sizing me up in the courtyard along with her crew, not you!" he said, finally putting two and two together.

"It sure wasn't me, 'cuz I don't hang out with *them*. Besides, I wasn't even at school last Friday," she said, making it clear to him that she didn't socialize with that bunch.

Lucas now realized that he had been rude to Kennedy for no reason. When he saw her in Starbucks, he had automatically assumed that it was Reagan. He started to apologize, but the teacher began talking, and he turned his attention to the front of the room.

"Now, class, open your books to page two-oh-four," Mrs. Vance instructed.

Kennedy cracked open her book, but kept her eyes glued on Lucas. He was so cute, and she wanted to run her hands through his curly hair. She had finally gotten his attention. Her only question now was: would he like her or her twin?

21

The moment the last bell of the day rang, Lucas bolted through the doors, on his way to the studio. En route to the subway, he took out his cell phone, and texted his boy Devin.

wht up?

After a few seconds, Devin responded, *Jst got n frm schl*

u wont bleve wht hppned 2day

wht

u no dat chck Ros frn

da 1 n strbks

yep. she got a twin!

WORD! Devin responded back in capital letters.

da 3 of us n da sme clss

word?

yep. i dissd her n strbks cz i thgt she hd dissd me, whn it ws her sster who dissd me

wht u gonna do now? U gonna date 'em both? Devin asked, spoken like a true player.

naw man! i gots 2 tell her im sorry. ddnt get a chnce 2 tll her n schl 2day.

u get her #

naw. 2 many nosey pp lsntin 4 me 2 ax

wht u gonna do

try & ctch her b4 clsses start 2mor

let me no wht hpns

k. ttyl

k

Lucas locked his phone and slid it back into his pocket. As he walked to the train station, he couldn't get the twins out of his mind. They were both drop-dead gorgeous, except one was down-to-earth, and one had her head so far in the stratosphere, that she thought that she was a star! He was so stunned by them, that he didn't even get a chance to ask the one in his chemistry group her name. He wanted to strike up a conversation after class, but Sid, the geek of the group, had her cornered, telling her not to forget to bring her homework assignment. They had caught each other's eye, but it wasn't the right time to get personal; besides, they both had another class to rush off to.

Kennedy was in her room working on the hypothesis for chemistry, but her mind kept wandering. She had caught Lucas giving her the eye, and couldn't help but wonder what he was thinking. He rushed out of class so fast that she didn't get a chance to flirt with him, not that she knew how to. *At least now he knows that I have a twin, and I'm not a part of Reagan's superficial crew,* she thought. Just as she was busy typing up her assignment, someone knocked at her door.

"Come in!" she yelled.

Reagan opened the door, waltzed in and looked around as if it were her first time in Kennedy's room. Unlike her girly-girl room with bright colors, posters of the latest boy band, and pictures torn from the pages of *Vogue* and *W* taped to the wall, Kennedy's was totally different. Her room was painted in muted tones of dove gray and white. Instead of the latest fashion spread, she had posters touting, *World Peace, Save the Environment,* and *End Hunger.* There wasn't one, not one picture of a boy anywhere in sight, not even the singer Mario, who was a complete BABE!

"What do you want?" Kennedy asked, as she watched her sister survey her room.

"Why do I have to want anything?"

"'Cuz you never come in here. So you must want something."

"So…" Reagan began, and then took a seat on one of Kennedy's twin beds. "What's with the new look?"

I knew she wanted something. She wants to know why I changed my hair, and bought new shoes, Kennedy thought as she studied her sister. "What new look?" she asked, toying with Reagan.

"You know—the hair, shoes, purse," she said cryptically.

"Yeah, what about 'em?"

"Look, Kennedy, why are you being such a wise ass? I'm simply asking, that's all," Reagan said, getting fed-up with her sister's smart comments.

"You never cared what I looked like before. All you cared about was that me and my ratty army jacket stayed far away from you and your designer-wearing friends."

"Speaking of the army jacket, what did you do with it?" she asked, totally ignoring Kennedy's comment.

"Why?"

"Because it was Uncle Percy's, and I wouldn't want to see it tossed out. He did serve in Vietnam with that jacket," Reagan said.

"Wow! I'm shocked you even know that. I thought you hated the jacket," Kennedy said, surprised that her sister knew some family history.

"I don't hate that jacket. It bugged me that you had to wear it every single day, like some sort of badge of honor."

"It was an honor to wear it. I mean our uncle nearly lost his life in Nam. I guess I was wearing it as a tribute to him."

"So why'd you stop?" Reagan asked, getting back to the original question.

"I have my reasons," was all Kennedy said. She and Reagan hadn't had a civil conversation in forever, and Kennedy was beginning to warm up to her sister, but she should have known that Reagan had ulterior motives for asking about the army jacket.

Reagan put her hand on her chin. "Really? What are they?"

"I should've known that you didn't care anything about the jacket. You only want to get in my business."

Reagan sprang off the bed. "You don't," she pointed her finger in Kennedy's face, "have any business that would interest me. I was merely trying to make conversation."

Kennedy wished that that were true. She wished that she and her sister were close like twins were supposed to be, and that she could tell Reagan about the crush she had on Lucas, but she couldn't. Kennedy didn't trust Reagan. When they were in elementary school, before the sibling rivalry was in full effect, Kennedy had a crush on a boy in their class, and the minute Reagan found out that the boy was interested in Kennedy, she set out to win him over. Reagan eventually won his affection, and the whole incident had left Kennedy devastated. From that point on, Kennedy distanced herself from Reagan, and never confided in her sister again.

"Look, Reagan, if you wouldn't mind," she gestured toward her computer, "I have to get back to work."

"Whatev!" Reagan flipped her long hair to one side, and stormed out.

Now all I have to do is make sure Lucas likes me, before Reagan gets her claws into him, Kennedy thought, before getting back to her homework assignment.

22

Lucas got to school early, and waited outside the gates for Kennedy to show up. He wanted to apologize for being so rude to her when they were at Starbucks. He leaned back on the stone wall with the earphones to his iPod stuck in his ears and listened to his new single. He bopped his head to the beat, and waited and watched. Though it was a private school, the girls all seemed to have their own style. Some wore their skirts short, others long. Some wore high-heels, while others wore flats. And they all seemed to carry designer purses, totes, or duffels. As Lucas watched the students file into the schoolyard, it occurred to him that he might not recognize his target. She and her sister looked so much alike, he was afraid that he would approach the wrong one. And no way was he giving an undue apology to the snobby twin.

I'll wait to see her in class. At least with her sitting across from me in chemistry, I'm sure not to make a case of mistaken identity, Lucas thought and abandoned his post by the gate.

Lucas' third and fourth periods dragged by. Finally, after what seemed like forever, he was entering chemistry class. He had rehearsed his speech in his first two classes, but the moment he sat at the lab bench, across from *her*, the words left his mind.

"Hi, uh, I'm Lucas Williams, but I never got your name," he said to Kennedy.

She was reading over the hypothesis, and didn't even hear—or see—him sit down. Kennedy looked up, and a smile sprang to her face. "Excuse me?"

"I asked you your name?"

"Oh, it's Kennedy Mercier."

"Mer-see-ay?" he said, pronouncing it phonetically. "That's an odd last name."

"It's Creole. My dad's family is from New Orleans," she explained.

"Oh," he said, staring into her warm brown eyes.

"Kennedy, I hope you have the hypothesis *today*," Sid said, interrupting their getting-to-know-you session.

"Yep, got it right here," she said, closing the folder, and handing it to her overzealous classmate.

"Hiii, Lucasss," Reese sang as she joined the group.

"Yeah, hey. What up?"

"Nothing yet." She winked her eye. "You wanna hang out after school?" she asked, and winked again.

"You got something in your eye?" he asked, ignoring her proposition.

"No, I don't have anything in my eye. Why?"

"'Cause you keep blinking."

Kennedy put her hand to her mouth, and giggled. She was used to seeing Reese work her magic on the cute boys in school, but she had never seen anyone shoot her down like Lucas had just done.

"Whatever!" Reese said, and flipped open her textbook.

Class started before Lucas could throw another insult Reese's way. With the teacher talking, he didn't want to interrupt class, but he also didn't want Kennedy to leave without apologizing to her. He flipped open his spiral, scribbled a note, tore the paper off the silver coil, folded it up and handed it to Kennedy.

Kennedy unfolded the paper, which said, *"I'm sorry about Starbucks."* She read it, but had no idea what it meant. She looked at Lucas and hunched her shoulders.

He scribbled another note, and handed it to her. *"Meet me after school by the front gates."*

Kennedy mouthed, *"Okay."*

Their little interchange didn't go unnoticed. Reese and Sid were ogling them, but they were not the only people in class watching; so were Reagan and her crew. They were paying more attention to Lucas and Kennedy than to the teacher.

"So what do you think the note said?" Madison whispered to Reagan.

"He probably wants to borrow her notes. I bet he's not too bright," Reagan responded.

"No. That's not it. He has to be smart in order to get into Walburton, scholarship or no scholarship."

"Yeah, you're right. He's probably asking her about me. Why would he want Kennedy when I'm a much better choice? Not that I'd ever have three words to say to his poor ass, except, 'Beat it, LOSER!'" Reagan said narcissistically, raising her voice slightly.

"Excuse me, Ms. Mercier, but if you have something more important to say, then I'll be more than happy to let you teach class today," Mrs. Vance said, catching Reagan in the act.

Reagan felt her face blush from embarrassment, and looked down at her textbook, as if she hadn't uttered a word.

"Don't get quiet on us now. A few minutes ago, you had plenty to say," the teacher said, further embarrassing Reagan. "Do you or do you not want to take over my job?"

"No," Reagan said, underneath her breath.

"Speak up, child!"

Kennedy wanted to bust out laughing. For once, the joke was on her sister, and she was glad. Reagan always seemed to get away with her snide remarks, but not this time. Kennedy looked over at Reagan, who had her head buried so far down her chest that it looked as if she didn't have a neck.

"No, I do not want to run the class," Reagan said, picking her head off her chest.

"I thought not. Now if you'll apologize for interrupting the class, we can get back to business."

"But I wasn't the only one talking!" Reagan said, nearly shouting. She hated being called out like that, and if she had to go down, she wasn't going alone.

Madison shot her a killer look.

Fed up with this unnecessary exchange, Mrs. Vance now had a nasty scowl painted on her face. "That may or may not be true. The truth of the matter is you are the one that I saw and heard, so it will be *you* that apologizes! Is that clear?"

"I'm sorry," Reagan said, so low that the words were barely audible.

"We can't hear you. Since you are having such a hard time projecting, I want you to come to the front of the class and apologize."

All eyes were on Reagan as she reluctantly made her way to the head of the class.

Standing front and center, she looked out at her classmates. Reagan glanced at her sister who had a smirk plastered across her face; she was no doubt enjoying the PDH (Public Display of Humiliation). And that new boy Lucas was staring at her, obviously waiting for her to say something. Next Reagan cast her eyes on Madison who looked pissed, with her arms folded tightly across her chest.

"Ms. Mercier, we are all waiting," Mrs. Vance said rather impatiently.

"I'm sorry for disturbing the class!" Reagan yelled, loud and clear, making sure that she was heard. She spoke so loud that she was sure the class next door also heard.

"Very well; you can take your seat now," Mrs. Vance said, satisfied with the apology.

Feeling like a loser, Reagan slunk back to her seat with her ego totally shattered.

The class resumed, and before long the bell rang. Lucas and Kennedy went their separate ways to their different classes. When school let out, Lucas resumed his post by the stone wall, outside of the gates, and waited for Kennedy to show up. He looked up and down the street, and noticed a beautiful silverish-blue Mercedes Maybach waiting in front of the school. *Damn, that car is BAD! I wonder who's rolling in THAT? One day I'm gonna have a whip like that,* Lucas thought as he admired the luxury ride.

Kennedy could see Lucas through the wrought-iron gates, and her heart began to pound faster. She didn't know why he wanted to see her after school, and the thought of it was making her nervous.

"Hey, Lucas." She smiled as she approached, trying to hide her nervousness.

He smiled back. "Hey, Kennedy. Uh…you wanna get something to drink?"

"Sure. There's this great old-fashioned deli around the corner. They have the best egg-creams."

"That sounds good."

"It's this way," she said, and started walking away from the school, with Lucas by her side.

They walked down the block, and around the corner.

The moment they stepped inside the deli, it was like stepping back in time. There was an antique glass pastry case in the front, displaying a variety of cannoli, cookies, brownies, and other delicious sweets. The booths were wooden, as were the tables and chairs. All the tables were topped with red-and-white, plaid cotton cloths, making the place look like a grandmother's cozy kitchen. There was even a wooden bar with an old-fashioned soda fountain.

"Sit anywhere you like," said the cashier standing behind the register near the door.

"Come on, let's sit at the bar. It's fun watching them make milkshakes and egg-creams," Kennedy said.

"Okay."

They walked over to the bar, and took seats on the chrome stools with the red leather seats.

"What can I get ya?" asked the guy behind the bar. He was wearing a red-and-white striped shirt and white, chef's-type hat.

"What are you going to have?" Lucas asked Kennedy.

"Hmm." She looked at the menu that was printed on the wall in front of her. "Let's see. I think I'm going to have a chocolate milkshake."

"I'll have the same," Lucas told the waiter. "I thought you would order the egg-cream, since you said they are so good here," he said to her once the waiter was gone.

"I was, but I'm more in the mood for a thick shake instead. Soo...Lucas, what was that note about?"

Being in this throw-back deli with Kennedy made him forget all about the note, and why he had asked to see her after school. "Oh, the note. I wanted to apologize for how rude I was to you at Starbucks."

Kennedy had been so surprised to see him that day, that she hadn't even noticed that he was being rude. "I didn't think you were acting rude. You rushed out of the place so fast, that I thought you really had to get home."

"The reason I left in a hurry was because I thought that you were talking about me in the courtyard that day. But it wasn't you; it was your sister," he explained.

"Oh, I see. Don't worry about it. Apology accepted."

"Speaking of your sister, Mrs. Vance really put her on blast today."

"Yeah, she finally got caught talking out of turn. Hey, you can consider her humiliation today as payback for her and her friends ragging on you," Kennedy said.

"Now that's an excellent thought!" He smiled, exposing his deep dimples.

As they were enjoying a laugh at Reagan's expense, the waiter brought over one gigantic milkshake topped high with a mound of whipped-cream and two cherries on top, in a beautifully etched glass with two extra-long straws sticking out of each side. "Since you two ordered the same thing, I thought I'd put it in one of our sharing glasses, like we used to do years ago. Enjoy," he said, and walked away.

Kennedy and Lucas looked at each other, and then at

the humongous shake. "Wow!" they said in unison, and then began sipping out of their respective straws.

Lucas looked over at Kennedy, and couldn't help but think how pretty she was. Not only was she *Phine* with a "Ph," she was also cool. Most chicks he knew wouldn't be caught dead in an old-fashioned deli, sharing a milkshake. No way! Girls these days were more interested in sucking down a Martini, trying to be grown. Kennedy obviously had morals, and he was digging that. *Coming to Walburton is turning out to be better than I thought.*

"So you think I can call you sometime?" he asked, coming up for air.

Kennedy nearly choked. She hadn't expected him to ask for her number so soon. "Sure!" She scribbled down her number on a napkin and gave it to him.

Lucas stuck the napkin in his pocket, and continued with the shake. He and Kennedy sat there facing each other, sipping the shake, and staring at each other. They looked like two love-struck kids from the fifties. The only things missing were bobby socks and a letter jacket!

23

Ian's parents were out of town *again*, and again he had his father's Maybach and driver. Initially, he had planned to just have him and his friends picked up from school and taken back to his penthouse, but after Reagan's tongue-lashing by Mrs. Vance, and Reagan then trying to share the blame with Madison, he sensed that the girls would be in a tainted mood, and need a diversion from the norm.

"I want to know why you tried to get me in trouble?" Madison asked Reagan once they were settled in the back of the car.

"It's not like I was the only one talking. As a matter of fact, *you* started the conversation in the first place!" Reagan huffed.

"At least I had the good sense to whisper," Madison retorted.

"Now, now, girls, let's not rehash the past. Let's get wasted instead," Ian said, opening the door to the mini-fridge.

"Sounds good to me!" PG chimed in, always eager to get his drink on.

Ian waited for Madison and Reagan to respond, but they just sat there with their arms folded across their chests. He had never seen them at odds before. Normally they were as thick as thieves. *Must be that time of the month for both of them*, he thought. "I think champagne is a good tension buster. How about I open some Cristal?" he said, reaching for the golden-labeled bottle.

At the mention of drinking the good stuff, both girls seemed to lighten up. Madison uncrossed her arms, and said, "I would love a glass."

"What about you, Reagan?" Ian asked.

"I could definitely use some champagne, especially after the day I've had," she said, almost back to her old self.

Ian took the gold foil off the bottle, unscrewed the wire, and twisted the cork off like a pro. He then poured four flutes of bubbly, and passed them around. "To us!" he toasted. And they all raised their glasses, like they were American royalty.

"Where are we going?" PG asked.

"I thought we'd give the penthouse a rest, and cruise around the city, maybe stop and get something to eat later," Ian told them.

"Sounds like a plan," PG said, gulping his champagne, and then pouring another glass.

"I can't stay out too late. I have an early-morning shoot," Madison said.

"You're not coming to school tomorrow?" Reagan

asked, speaking to Madison civilly for the first time since class.

"Yeah, I'm going, just taking the morning off. Nancy has already arranged for me to miss the morning classes. She even got the homework assignments faxed to her house."

"Your grandmother is something else," Reagan said.

"Tell me about it. I could surely use a break from her spying," Madison said sounding glum, as if her grandmother was the Gestapo.

Hearing the sadness in Madison's voice, Ian thought of the perfect solution to her woes. "I have an idea, Mad," he said, putting his hand on her knee.

"What's that?" Madison asked.

"Since my parents are going to be out of town for the next two weeks, why don't you come over on Friday, and spend the night?" he asked, eager to put his plan into motion.

Madison quickly glanced at Reagan, who was giving her a raised eyebrow look. Madison had been recently thinking about sleeping with Ian, but she didn't expect him to ask her to stay over in front of their friends. She wanted to say yes, but didn't want to seem easy in front of PG. She wasn't worried about Reagan, since they had talked about doing the "deed" before. "Uh, I don't know. Call me later, and I'll tell you what I decided," she said, finding the perfect answer.

Damn it, why didn't I wait to ask her when she was alone!

Ian thought, afraid that he had blown his chances. "Of course, sweetie, anything you want." He smiled.

Reagan couldn't believe that Ian had propositioned Madison in front of her and PG, but it was just like a boy not to have any decorum. She hoped that PG wasn't getting any ideas of his own. He was the last person she wanted to sleep with. Reagan had planned for the boy who popped her cherry to be FINE—RICH and FINE!

"Mad, I got a flier in the mail yesterday from Barneys. The new Juicy Couture line is out. You wanna check it out with me?" Reagan asked, trying to offer her friend an olive branch.

"Yeah, sure."

"Look, Mad, I'm sorry for trying to get you in trouble with Mrs. Vance," Reagan said, finally apologizing.

"No problem, Rea, but next time she catches you, leave me out of it, okay?"

"Hopefully, there won't be a next time. But, okay."

The group rode around the city drinking two-hundred-dollar bottles of champagne, laughing and talking like they didn't have a care in the world. Now that Reagan and Madison had made up, their little clique was back to normal. The only pressing matter was whether or not Madison was going to take Ian up on his offer!

24

Today was Lucas' big day! *106 & Park* was debuting his new video, as well as interviewing him. Kevin wanted to pick him up after school, but Lucas declined. He didn't want the other students seeing him get into a limo. Lucas thought back to the other day when he saw that "sick" Maybach waiting outside of the school. These kids were so rich that a measly Town Car probably wouldn't even faze them. Besides, he didn't want to fire up the rumor mill with talk about him being chauffeur driven. So after school, Lucas took the subway to the BET studio for his "close-up."

"Hey, man," Kevin greeted Lucas as he walked through the lobby.

"Hey, Kevin." Lucas smiled in return.

"Is your mom coming in for the taping?" Kevin asked.

"Naw, she has inventory at the store and can't get away."

"Oh, I see," he said, sounding a little disappointed. "I thought that since she came to the video shoot, that she'd be here for your first on-camera interview," Kevin explained.

"She wanted to come, but I told her it wasn't necessary. I'm not a little boy who needs hand-holding."

"No. You're far from a little boy. You're nearly a man. Besides, you have a good head on your shoulders, and I know you'll be great in front of the camera. Don't be nervous; just be yourself. I told them not to ask too many personal questions."

"Thanks, Kevin, 'cause I wasn't looking forward to talking about my upbringing, and how my moms had to struggle after my pops died," Lucas said, with a tinge of sadness in his voice.

"Don't worry about that. I told them to mainly focus on the music. Now they are going to ask if you have a girlfriend. Because your adoring fans will want to know." Kevin smiled.

Kennedy flashed across Lucas's mind. She wasn't his girlfriend, but he did like her, and hoped that if she saw his interview, she wouldn't be offended by his candor. "No problem. I got it covered, Guru."

Kevin laughed when Lucas call him a Guru, then said, "Good. Now, let's check in and head to the Green Room so you can change out of your uniform, into this outfit I bought you," Kevin said, holding up a garment bag.

Once they passed security, they made their way to the Green Room, where Lucas gladly changed from his nerdy khakis, white oxford shirt, boring tie, and blue blazer.

"Now you look like the star I know you are!" Kevin beamed.

"Thanks, man! I'm digging these Mavi jeans," Lucas

said, turning around in the full-length mirror. "And this shirt is dope!" he said, commenting on the black Hugo Boss fitted shirt.

"You're welcome. Come on, let's get to makeup," Kevin told him, opening the door and heading down the hall.

Lucas was so cute that he didn't need much makeup to enhance his looks; all he needed was a little dusting powder on his forehead and nose to get rid of his natural sheen, and then he was camera ready.

"Wow, you look better in person than you do on your CD cover. The girls in the audience today are going to eat you alive!" the associate producer said, walking into the makeup room.

Lucas blushed. "Thanks."

"Now here's the rundown…after the hosts give their opening, they're going to bring you out, and chat with you about your new CD, then play the video, and chat with you some more. It shouldn't take more than ten minutes. You have any questions?"

"No, I'm straight."

"Great! Okay, let's get over to the set," she said, leading the way.

Lucas could hear the live studio audience stirring around as they neared the studio. The nerves that had eluded him earlier were now beginning to creep into his body, making his hands shake. *Calm down! Just pretend like you're talking to Devin. Stop trippin', it's only an interview!* he scolded himself.

"We're going to wait right here," the producer said,

stopping right outside the entrance to the set. "Wait for me to give you the cue to enter. Okay?"

"Okay." Lucas nodded his head, and listened to the action inside the studio.

"We have a great show today; not only are we going to play some of your favorite videos," the male host said. "But we're also debuting a new joint by Lucas Williams, a hot new singer/rapper, and, ladies, he is FINE!" the female host said, revving up the audience.

Lucas, Kevin and the producer could hear clapping and cheers from where they stood.

"Now all that excitement is a good sign!" the producer commented.

After a few videos played, the female host said, "Okay, ladies, are you ready to meet Lucas?!"

"Yeah!!!" the females in the audience yelled collectively.

The producer tapped Lucas on the arm, and mouthed, "Go now."

Lucas strolled onstage with his swagger in full effect. The walk wasn't thuggish; it was a junior Denzel, sexy-type strut. As Lucas made his way toward the hosts, the girls in the audience were on their feet clapping and screaming his name. He couldn't believe the impact that he was having simply by walking onstage. Lucas couldn't help but grin at the love that he was getting from the audience.

"Man, you got the babes going crazy, and they haven't even seen your video yet," the male host said.

"Okay, since y'all can't wait, we're going to play his video right now," the female host chimed in.

The hosts escorted Lucas to the sofa to get set up for the interview while his video aired. Lucas watched the screen along with everyone else, and couldn't believe that he was watching himself. It was a surreal feeling, as if he were watching someone else perform. He didn't want to sound like an egomaniac, but he had to admit that he looked and sang like an old pro. After the video was over, the questions began.

"Lucas, that was hot! How did you come up with the concept of shooting on a rooftop with the city in the background?"

"Actually, it was my producer's idea, and I went with it."

"Not only are you a great singer, but you can dance your butt off!" the female host said.

"Yeah, your moves remind me a little of Chris Brown," the male host added.

"Thanks, I consider that a high compliment," Lucas answered graciously.

"When is the CD dropping?" asked the male host.

"Next Tuesday."

"With this hot video, I'm sure your single is going to shoot straight up the charts," the female host said.

"Yeah, we'll see," Lucas answered modestly, not wanting to toot his own horn.

"Sooo…Lucas…," the female host said, pinning him with a death stare, "…do you have a girlfriend?"

"Naw." He blushed. "I'm single."

"That's good to know," she said, sounding like she was interested in dating the young star.

"Okay, enough about his availability. Let's get back to the music. How did you get discovered, Lucas?" the male host asked.

Lucas told them all about his high school talent show, and how Kevin was in the audience and was impressed by Lucas's singing skills, and offered him a recording contract.

"Are you working on your sophomore album?"

"Not yet. Right now, we're concentrating on promoting this CD," Lucas told them.

After a few more questions, the interview was over.

"Lucas, thanks for coming on the show, and we wish you all the best with your career," the male host said, ending the interview.

"Man, that was awesome! You handled yourself like a real pro!" Kevin congratulated Lucas once he left the set.

"Thanks, Kevin. It was exciting!" Lucas grinned. "When is it going to air?"

"I'll find out the exact date from the producer, and let you know. Now, come on; let me buy you dinner. How about some soul food?" Kevin asked.

"Sounds good to me!"

They left the studios, jumped in the waiting Town Car and drove uptown to Sylvia's, Harlem's legendary soul food restaurant. After a meal of smothered chicken, collard greens, macaroni and cheese, hot-buttered biscuits and homemade peach cobbler for dessert, Kevin dropped Lucas off in front of his door.

The apartment was dark and quiet, when Lucas stepped inside. He presumed that his mother was still at work doing inventory, so he went to his room to unwind.

"Man, what a day!" he said aloud as he plopped down on his bed, and untied his shoes. Not only had he put in a full day at school, he also had done his first television interview!

He was still pumped, and started to call Devin to tell him all about being on *106 & Park*, but decided not to. Devin wasn't the person he wanted to talk to at the moment. Lucas got up from the bed, went to his dresser and picked up the napkin that Kennedy had given him with her phone number on it. He went back to the bed and sat down. He looked at the number trying to decide whether or not to call her. He wanted to talk to her, but at the same time he was starting to feel nervous.

"What the hell?" he said, and began dialing her number from his cell phone.

"Hello?" she answered.

"Hey, Kennedy, it's Lucas; what you up to?"

"Oh, hey Lucas!" she said, sounding happy to hear from him. "Nothing much; just finished my homework. What are you up to?"

Lucas quickly thought whether or not he should tell Kennedy about his singing career. *She's cool, I don't think she's going to trip out about it. Besides, the video will be air-ing soon, and she's going to find out anyway, so I might as well tell her.* "Uh...I did an interview after school today."

"An interview? What type of interview?"

"I'm a singer and rapper," he said modestly.

"Really, are you in a group with your friends?" she asked, assuming that he was an amateur.

"No, I'm solo."

"Oh, was the interview for a local paper?" she asked, still not catching on.

"Naw, it was on BET," he said with a humble tone to his voice, trying to downplay the situation.

"BET!!" she shouted. "Are you kidding?"

"Naw, I'm going to be on *106 & Park*. They're debuting my new video."

"What?! Your new video? So I take it you have a recording contract," she said, finally putting two and two together.

"Yeah, I do."

"Having a recording contract and being featured on BET is a huge deal, but you sound so calm about it!"

"Don't get me wrong, I am extremely excited. It's just that I want to keep everything in perspective. That's why I didn't say anything at the deli. I want to make sure people like me for who I am, and not for what I do."

"That's a good philosophy. But wait until after your video and interview air; you're going to have more new friends than you know what to do with."

"I'm not interested in those types of friends. My circle is small and I'd like to keep it that way."

"I know what you mean. I don't have many friends either, which suits me fine," Kennedy said.

"I know we just met, but I hope you count me as one of your friends," Lucas said boldly.

"For sure!" Kennedy said, nearly singing into the receiver.

"Good. You wanna go to the movies this weekend?" he asked.

"I'd like that."

Lucas heard his mom come into the apartment, and he wanted to tell her all about his interview, so he cut the conversation short. "Okay, Kennedy, I'll see you in school tomorrow."

"Okay. Good night, Lucas."

"Good night, Kennedy," he said, and hung up.

Lucas lay back on his pillows, and replayed the day over in his mind, before going to talk to his mother. Although it was exciting to be on BET, the favorite part of his day was talking to Kennedy. Her voice was so pleasant that it made him feel good inside. He didn't know that much about girls, but he knew that he liked Kennedy—a lot—and couldn't wait to get to know her better!

25

It was Saturday afternoon, and Madison couldn't wait to get home and call Reagan to tell her all about Friday night! Madison knew that her mother would be at the neighborhood park with her little brother, so the moment she bolted through the front door of their apartment, she made a beeline straight to her bedroom, and locked the door for extra security just in case her mom came home early. She kicked off her shoes, threw her overnight bag on the bed, propped herself on the cushioned window seat that overlooked Central Park, and called her best friend.

"What took you so long? I've been waiting by the phone all morning," Reagan spat into the receiver the second she picked up the phone.

"Sorry. I just walked through the door."

"So, how did it go? Tell me everything, and don't leave out a single detail."

"Thursday night, Ian called and asked me again if I would spend the night at his apartment Friday, and—"

"And obviously you said yes," Madison butted in.

"Yeah, but first I needed an alibi, and when I told Ian that, he suggested I tell my mother I'd be spending the night with you. So that's what I told her to get out of the house," Madison said.

"Omigod!" Reagan shrieked. "Why didn't you tell me that you were using me as your alibi? Suppose your mother had called here, and wanted to speak with you? That would have been disastrous!"

"I know; luckily she didn't. I had every intention of calling you, but I got so caught up trying to decide what to bring to his apartment that I nearly stayed up half the night and then the other half of the night, I tossed and turned with anticipation. I didn't get any sleep, so Friday at school I was a walking zombie, and totally forgot to tell you. Sorry," Madison said.

"Okay, enough with the preliminaries. What happened when you got to the penthouse?" Reagan asked, ready to hear the juicy details.

"We drank as usual, except this time, instead of two pomegranate martinis, I had at least five. I was so tipsy, that by the time he carried me off to his bedroom, I was wasted."

"You mean he literally picked you up and carried you into his bedroom, like in the movies?" Reagan asked, in awe.

Madison nodded her head up and down even though Reagan couldn't see her, and said, "Yep."

"Wow, how romantic! So, what happened next?"

"He laid me on the bed, got on top of me, and started kissing me, like there was no tomorrow."

"So did you use the condoms that you bought?"

"No, I—"

"YOU DIDN'T USE ANY PROTECTION!" Reagan shrieked into the phone.

"Wait a minute; you didn't give me a chance to finish. We didn't use protection, because I passed out."

"What do you mean, you passed out?"

"I mean that I got so drunk that I literally passed out while Ian was grinding on top of me! I guess it was a combination of too much alcohol and too little food. Anyway, when I woke up this morning, I had a massive hangover, and wasn't in the mood to do much of anything except drink a pot of coffee, and eat a plate of eggs, bacon, and toast. But we couldn't have done anything if we had wanted to, because Ian's maid had come into work early in the morning, and I surely wasn't about to spread my legs while she was roaming around the penthouse," Madison said.

"Wow, that's some story! It's not the story that I was expecting, but it was entertaining just the same."

"Glad I could be your amusement this afternoon," Madison said.

"Don't get huffy with me because you passed out."

"I'm not getting huffy; it's just that I'm a little frustrated. I was really looking forward to losing my virginity, and finding out what all the hoopla is about. At the next photo shoot, I wanted to be able to chime in when the conversation turned to sex," Madison said, sounding disappointed.

"Don't worry. I'm sure Ian will be hounding you to stay over again. And next time, don't forget to clue me in, if you're going to use me as your alibi."

"I won't. Wait, I think I heard my mother and brother come in. Let me go before she overhears my conversation," Madison said.

"Okay, I'll talk to you later."

When Madison got off the phone, she began unpacking her overnight bag. She took out a sexy black negligee that she had bought at La Perla, a bottle of Dolce & Gabbana Light Blue cologne, and the box of condoms that she had bought at the drug store. She opened her bottom dresser drawer, and stuffed everything in the back of the drawer except the perfume, which she put on top of the dresser.

Hopefully next time I'll be able to break the seal on the condoms and put them to good use, Madison thought as she stared out the window and across the street into the park.

26

Madison had passed out before Ian could pop her cherry. He was pissed, but wasn't about to screw dead weight. He was horny, not desperate! All of his planning had gone down the drain—well, not literally down the drain since she hadn't thrown up. Ian wanted to loosen Madison up with a few drinks, but their drinking escalated until they were both drunk. He was more tipsy than drunk, but Madison had gone over the edge to Never Never Land.

Next time, only two drinks for Ms. Reynolds, Ian thought as he sat down in front of his computer.

Ian had sent Magdala home early so that he could have the place to himself. He was still horny, and knew exactly what to do to scratch his itch.

Ian logged onto his computer, turned on the webcam, and went to his favorite website. *There's more than one way to skin a cat*, he mused as he waited for the site to upload.

Then with a few clicks on the keyboard, he was in business! Presto! Just like that!! Oh, how Ian loved cyberspace!

27

Kennedy had showered, and was now back in her bedroom trying to decide what to wear. She had gone shopping earlier that day, and now had several outfits spread out on the bed. One was casual chic with a pair of Juicy Couture black stretch denims and a white beaded Rocawear tunic. The other outfit was more casual with a pair of Miss Sixty jeans, and a lavender hoodie by Ed Hardy.

She stood back and surveyed her goods. The black jeans were a bit too dressy for the movies, so she chose the blue jeans instead, and the white tunic.

Kennedy started to flatiron her hair but she didn't really feel like it. Besides, Lucas didn't seem impressed when she had done it before, so she let her natural locks flow freely.

She had finished dressing, and was slipping on her cork-heeled wedges, another new purchase, when she heard a knock at the door.

"Come in!" Kennedy yelled.

The door creaked opened, and in came Reagan. This

time, instead of surveying the room like she had done before, Reagan studied her sister. Her eyes were like tiny laser beams, zeroing in on every inch of Kennedy's body. "When did you get those shoes? I saw them in Neiman's catalog," Reagan finally said.

"Oh these Miss Sixty wedges?" Kennedy said, pointing her toe like a ballerina. "I ordered them from the Neiman Marcus website to go with my new Miss Sixty jeans that I bought today," she said, twirling around so that Reagan could get the full effect.

Reagan's jaw dropped. She didn't know that Kennedy was hip to the latest designers, let alone where to buy them. Kennedy had never shown any real interest in shopping before; now it was like her sister was being possessed by the fashion editors of *Vogue*, *Mademoiselle*, or *Glamour*, or maybe all three. The jeans accentuated the curve of her hips, and the top showed off her collar bone perfectly. She looked like a model, except for her unruly hair.

"Soo…where are you going all dolled-up like that?" Reagan asked.

"Out," Kennedy simply said.

"Okay, Ms. Smarty Pants, I can see that. Who are you going out with?" Reagan asked, refusing to drop the subject.

Kennedy thought for a second, trying to decide if she should tell Reagan that she was going on a date with Lucas. Then she decided, why not? He had made it clear that he wasn't interested in Reagan. "I'm going to the movies with Lucas."

"Lucas?" Reagan asked, scrunching up her face.

"You know, the new guy in our chemistry class."

"*Him!* Why are you going out with that loser?" Reagan asked, as if Lucas were pond scum.

"He's *not* a loser!" Kennedy said, raising her voice and coming to his defense.

Reagan put her hand on her hip. "If he's not a loser, why is he at Walburton on a scholarship?"

"Who told you he was there on a scholarship?"

"It doesn't take a rocket scientist to figure that one out. Look at his uniform. It's too big, like it was donated or something," Reagan explained, making her case.

Kennedy had a good mind to tell her that Lucas was a singer and rapper, and that his new video was going to be aired on BET, but she decided not to. Besides, Reagan probably wouldn't believe her anyway, and if she did believe her, knowing Reagan, she'd be all over Lucas at school on Monday, trying to lure him away. Not telling Reagan was the best way to go, so Kennedy said, "Whatever."

"Have a good time with your loser," she said, putting up her fingers, making an "L" out of her thumb and index finger. "If that's even possible." She laughed and walked out.

"You're laughing now, but trust me, I'm going to get the last laugh," Kennedy said, underneath her breath.

As Kennedy was applying a thin coat of lip gloss, her cell rang.

"Hello?"

"Hey, Kennedy, are you ready?" asked Lucas.

"Just about."

"Good. What's your address?"

Kennedy told him where she lived.

"Okay, I'll be out front in fifteen minutes," he told her.

"Sounds good. See you then."

Kennedy ended the call, put the tiny phone in her purse, and danced around the room. This was her first real date, and she couldn't have been happier. For once she was the one going out on a Saturday night instead of her sister, and she was thrilled to no end. Kennedy completed the finishing touches, grabbed her purse and a jacket, and raced downstairs to wait for her date.

Lucas arrived exactly fifteen minutes later. Like a true gentleman, he was right on time.

"Wow, you look great!" he said, complimenting Kennedy on her outfit.

"Thanks." She blushed.

"Since the theater around the corner is playing that new horror flick, I thought we'd walk over there and check it out. You do like horror movies, don't you?"

"Yeah, I love 'em. The gorier the better."

"Excellent! Some chicks are too squeamish about all the blood and guts."

"That's so not me. I'm tougher than I look." She smiled.

"Okay, Ms. Tough, let's get going so we can get some good seats," Lucas said, leading the way.

They rounded the corner and headed for the Cineplex on Broadway. Once inside, Lucas stepped up to the window, and bought them tickets.

"You want some popcorn or candy?" he asked.

"For sure! What's a movie without popcorn and Raisinets?"

"That's what I'm talking about. Most chicks are so afraid of getting fat that they don't eat much, let alone buttery popcorn and chocolate-covered raisins."

"Again, I'm not like most chicks. I don't know how many times I have to keep telling you that," she said, poking him in the side with her elbow.

Lucas pulled Kennedy to him and wrapped his arm around her shoulders. "Yeah, I'm beginning to notice."

After stopping at the concession counter to fuel up, they headed into the theater.

"Where do you like sitting?" Lucas asked her.

"It doesn't matter."

"How about right here in the back," he said, gesturing toward two seats. "That way there'll be nobody screaming at our backs, or throwing popcorn over our shoulders."

"Makes sense," Kennedy said, making her way into the row.

As they waited for the previews to start, Lucas decided to ask Kennedy about Reagan. He found it odd how a set of twins could be so different, and wanted to know why. "So, why don't you and your sister get along?"

Kennedy sighed. "It's a long story. I don't even know where to begin."

"Start at the beginning."

"If you want to go back that far, you could say that it all started when our parents named us."

"What do you mean?"

"I was named Kennedy after my mother's favorite president, and Reagan was named after my father's favorite president. If you know your history, you know that those presidents were complete opposites. President Kennedy was a liberal Democrat, while President Reagan was a conservative Republican," she explained.

"Okay, that explains the names, but from what I've seen, your sister is anything but conservative."

"This is true, but have you ever heard of the 'Excess Eighties'? President Reagan was said to have instituted the overspending of the nineteen-eighties," Kennedy explained. "My sister surely has the spending part down. She buys more clothes than anybody I know."

"Oh, like you don't go shopping," Lucas said, ribbing her.

Kennedy popped a handful of popcorn in her mouth. "Yeah, I shop, but I'm not addicted to it."

"So, you and your sister have different spending ethics; that's not such a big deal. What else drove you two apart?" he asked, trying to learn more.

Kennedy started to tell Lucas about Reagan stealing her boyfriend, but she decided not to. She didn't want to come off like a whiner. "Let's see...I'm into saving the environment, and she's into what? Oh, that's right, nothing but herself."

Just then, the previews started, and the lights dimmed.

"Okay, I get the picture," Lucas whispered.

Kennedy was relieved that the previews had begun, because she was tired of talking about Reagan. This was her date, not her sister's. Now that Lucas knew the difference between them, he would never get them mixed up—or would he?

28

After their date on Saturday, Lucas and Kennedy agreed to meet early in the courtyard at school on Monday. Lucas was already there by the time Kennedy arrived. She was running late because she had taken too much time flat-ironing her hair. Saturday night she didn't mind wearing her hair wild, since her outfit was so fly, but today she wanted to compensate for the boring uniform.

"Hey there," Lucas said, as Kennedy approached him. He gave her an appraising stare. "Your hair is different today."

"Yeah, it is." She smiled, glad that he'd noticed.

"I like it. Not that I didn't like how you rocked your natural look Saturday night. What did you do differently?" Lucas asked, out of curiosity.

"I flat ironed it."

"What's a flatiron?"

"It's like a curling iron, but instead of a round barrel, it's flat so that it can straighten the hair better."

"Man, I can't believe you just explained that. Most girls would never reveal that type of insider information."

"It's not like this is some top secret information straight from the Pentagon." Kennedy put her hand on her hip. "Besides, how many times do I have to tell you that I'm not like most girls?"

"Yeah, yeah, yeah." He playfully poked her in the side. "I heard that before."

Kennedy poked him back with her elbow. "Well, act like it, and stop trying to group me with those other losers you date."

"You're the only loser I date." He laughed, and then grabbed her and put her in a mock headlock.

As they were fooling around with each other, Reagan, Madison, Ian and PG were standing in their usual spot eyeballing Lucas and Kennedy.

"My, my, aren't they acting buddy, buddy?" Madison said.

"Yeah, they're buddy, buddy alright. They went out on a date Saturday night," Reagan told them.

"How did that happen? Didn't they just meet?" PG asked.

"I guess losers gravitate toward each other," Reagan added.

They all broke out laughing at the snide remark.

"Look at them over there. I'd bet good money that they are getting their kicks off of us," Kennedy said, glaring at Reagan and her friends.

"They can laugh all they want. Trust me, when my record drops, they won't be laughing for long," Lucas said, with confidence.

"At that point, they'll be too busy trying to be your friend to make fun of you."

"Friends like that I don't need. Anyway, enough about them; what are you doing after school?"

"I'm going uptown for my Green Gardens meeting."

"I'm going uptown, too. Meet me here by the gate and we can ride the subway together."

Just then, the morning bell rang.

"Okay," Kennedy said, as they made their way inside.

Even though they were only riding the train together, Kennedy couldn't wait until school let out, so that she could spend more time with Lucas. Though she saw him in class, it wasn't the same. At least on the train they would have a chance to talk without nosey Reese and Sid listening to their every word. When the final bell of the day rang, Kennedy went straight to the girls' bathroom to change out of her uniform, comb her hair, and dab on some lip gloss. She then hurried outside, but Lucas wasn't there, so she waited at the designated spot.

Five minutes later, he came strolling up. "Sorry I'm late, but I had to take off that monkey suit."

Kennedy took one look at him and bit her bottom lip. Lucas looked so good in his jeans and a T-shirt that stretched across his chest showing off his muscles. Underneath the baggy uniform, his physique was lost, but the street clothes defined his toned body perfectly. She decided not to comment on how good he looked. She didn't want to blow his head up, so she simply said, "I hate those uniforms, too; they're so boring."

"Now that's another thing we have in common." He smiled.

"You keeping score?" she joked.

"Yeah, and lucky for you, your marks are acceptable."

"Whatever," she said, and flipped her hair in a dramatic gesture.

"Come on, girl, let's get to the train."

As they walked to the subway, Kennedy felt totally happy. Not only had she found a boy who liked her, he was fun to be with, and wasn't pretentious like most of the other kids who went to Walburton. Even though Lucas was a rising star, he was as down to earth as she was.

The train was packed, and they had to push their way on. Lucas led the way and found a tiny spot for them to stand near the back of the train.

"My manager texted me earlier and said that the release party for my new CD is Friday night," Lucas said, as he held onto the overhead pole.

"Oh, that's great! Are you excited?"

"Yeah, I am. I can't wait until the single starts playing on the radio, and the video is in constant rotation on BET. Uh…"—he looked down at his feet for a second, and looked back up—"you wanna go to the party with me?" he asked, totally changing the subject.

Kennedy felt her knees buckle. She knew it wasn't from the bumpy train ride, but from being asked to attend a record industry event with the boy of her dreams. She was speechless.

"You wanna go or not?" Lucas asked again, since she hadn't answered him yet.

"I would love to go!" Kennedy blurted.

"Good. I'll be riding in style that night, instead of on a crowded train, so I'll pick you up around seven."

"Okay," was all Kennedy managed to say, since she was still in a state of semi-shock.

A few stops later, they were in Harlem. Lucas grabbed her hand, and led the way off the train. When they reached street level, he was still holding her hand, and Kennedy didn't object. Even though Lucas hadn't officially asked her to be his girlfriend, she felt as if they were in a relationship. Especially since he had asked her to go to an important event with him, whether they were officially or unofficially dating, Kennedy really didn't care as long as he wanted to spend time with her.

"Hey, guys, wait up!" It was Ro, yelling from behind.

Kennedy and Lucas both turned around, and waited for her to catch up.

Ro took one look at their locked hands, and said, without hesitation, "What? So y'all a couple now?"

"What's it to you?" Lucas said, still holding onto Kennedy's hand.

"Don't get all huffy with me. I'm simply asking, that's all."

"So, Ro, what's been going on?" Kennedy asked, changing the subject. She didn't want to take the chance and hear Lucas say, "No, we're not dating."

Ro looked at their hand-lock once again, but didn't press any further; it was obvious that they were digging each other, so she let it go. "I got the best news over the weekend!" she said excitedly.

"Really, what?" Kennedy asked.

"I got a letter from the admissions department at Walburton, and guess what?" she asked, but didn't wait for an answer. "I finally got in! I'll be going there when the new school year starts!" she said, completely over-joyed.

"Wow, Ro, that's fantastic! I know how much you've wanted to get in," Kennedy said.

"Now we'll all be at the same school, and I can't wait!" Ro said.

Suddenly Kennedy thought about Reagan and her crew, and how shitty they were going to treat Roshonda. They would no doubt shun her like they did everyone who didn't live up to their pretentious standards. But Kennedy wasn't worried about Ro, since Ro could more than handle them. It then occurred to Kennedy that with Roshonda and Lucas both at Walburton, she'd have her own crew for once, and would no longer be an outsider!

29

"We'll each have the salmon, cooked medium rare, broccoli rabe, and a side of quinoa," Renée Reynolds—aka Nancy—told the waiter.

"Would you care for something else to drink besides bottled water?" he asked.

"No, Evian will be fine," she said, speaking for herself as well as her granddaughter.

Madison didn't want a healthy meal of fish, vegetables and grains; she wanted an iced-cold martini, and a juicy burger with extra cheese, but of course both of those items were off limits as far as her grandmother was concerned. Renée had summoned Madison to dinner to go over her upcoming schedule. At first Madison was excited since they were going to that new restaurant off Park Avenue. She had been dying to go there ever since they opened two months ago. But once they were seated and her grandmother started ordering for her, Madison regretted being there. The menu sounded delicious, with rare cuts of beef served in rich sauces, free-range chicken on a bed of smashed Yukon gold potatoes, and decadent desserts, but Renée had Madison on dietary restrictions, and wouldn't let her order anything remotely fattening.

"I spoke with your agent this afternoon, and she has some really interesting shoots lined up for you. She also sent your portfolio over to Tom Ford, and he wants to use you in his upcoming show, and is even thinking about hiring you to be his spokesmodel," Renée said, once the waiter was gone.

"Wow, that's great! I love Tom Ford's designs. He's awesome."

"Yes, he is extremely talented. I told her that you'd be pleased. She also set up a personal appearance for you."

"What type of personal appearance?" Madison asked. She was used to doing fashion shows, and magazine spreads with photographers, but she had never done an appearance.

"There's this young new singer that is having a release party for his upcoming album, and your agent and I both thought that it would be a good idea for you to attend. There's going to be media from across the country there, and it'll give you exposure beyond the fashion industry," Renée explained.

Madison couldn't believe her ears. Her overprotective grandmother had arranged for her to attend a hot party. Madison was getting excited, but calmed down. *There must be a catch*, she thought, and decided to find out more about this party before she got all hyped up. "So, who is the artist?"

"His name is Lucas Williams. Have you heard of him?"

"Lucas Williams?" Madison thought for a second. "That name does sound familiar."

"Maybe you read about him in one of those teen magazines," Renée said, trying to help jog Madison's memory.

"No, that's not it." Madison put her elbow on the table, and rested her chin in the palm of her hand. "Hmm, Lucas Williams, Lucas Williams," she said, repeating his name over and over. Then a hundred-watt bulb went off. "OMIGOD!"

"What is it, Dear?" Renée asked, sounding alarmed at Madison's loud tone.

"I know Lucas!"

"Really? Is he one of your school friends?"

"Yes, and no," Madison said cryptically.

"What do you mean, dear?"

"He goes to Walburton, but we're not exactly friends," she said, remembering how she had treated him on his first day. "Excuse me, Nancy. I have to go to the ladies' room," Madison said, getting up from the table with her purse in hand.

"Sure, dear."

Inside the restroom, Madison went straight to the suite—the large handicap stall—closed the door, hung her Jacobs bag on the door hook, dug out her cell phone and promptly called Reagan.

"Hey, Mad, I thought you were having dinner with Nancy this evening," Reagan said, once she picked up.

"I am, but I made a dash to the ladies' room. I had to call you," Madison whispered, covering the mouthpiece of the phone with her right hand, so she wouldn't be heard, just in case someone was in the next stall.

"What's going on? Why are you whispering?"

"You won't believe what I just learned!"

"What?" Reagan asked, sounding anxious.

"You know that new boy who goes to Walburton?"

"You mean the broke loser?" Reagan answered.

"Yes, him. But he's not a 'broke loser.'"

"What makes you think that? He's at Walburton on a scholarship, *and* he's dating Kennedy, so in my book, that makes him a *broke loser*!" she said, putting emphasis on the words. "Besides…"

Madison cut her off, "Hold on, there's something that you don't know."

"Look, I know all I need to know about Mr. BL," she said, giving him a nickname.

"No, you don't. Now if you'll stop talking, I'll tell you what I found out," Madison said, quieting her friend.

"Go ahead. I'm listening," Reagan said, sounding slightly annoyed that Madison had rudely cut her off.

"Lucas is a singer!" Madison shrieked underneath her breath.

"A singer?" Reagan asked, not sure if she had heard right.

"Yep, and get this…he's having a release party and my agent set me up to make an appearance."

"What? Are you sure it's the same boy who goes to

our school?" Reagan asked, still not believing what Madison was telling her.

"Yeah, I'm sure. Nancy just finished telling me."

"Maybe he just has the same name as this new singer."

"Hey, I've got an idea. Are you near your computer?" Madison asked.

"Yeah, I'm sitting at my desk right now."

"Google Lucas Williams, and see what comes up," Madison suggested.

"That's a good idea." A few clicks later, and Reagan yelled, "OMIGOD! OMIGOD!"

"What? What?"

"It's, it's him!! I can't believe it!"

"What does it say?"

Reagan read in silence for a moment, then said, "There's a picture of him standing on a rooftop looking sexy as hell, and it says his new CD is coming out next Tuesday, and that a huge party is scheduled for Friday to celebrate the release."

"See, I told you!"

"Omigod!" Reagan said, again, letting the information sink in.

"I can't believe that we were so rude to him. And I even asked if he was at Walburton on a scholarship."

"We both thought that he was there on a scholarship. If we had known that he was a potential star, then we would've insisted that he join our clique," Reagan said, sounding remorseful.

"I guess we blew that."

"Not really; maybe there's still a chance to win him over. I mean, if he likes Kennedy, then why wouldn't he like me? I mean, we do look exactly alike. Besides, I already took one boyfriend from her, so why not take this one, too?!" Reagan said, sounding heartless.

"And how are you going to manage that? Lucas doesn't even look in your direction."

"I don't know yet, but trust me, I'll think of something."

"Look, Rea, I gotta go before Nancy thinks I went AWOL, and comes storming in here looking for me."

"Okay. I'll talk to you later."

Madison put her phone back in her purse, exited the stall, and washed her hands. She didn't know what type of scheme Reagan was cooking up, but knowing her friend, whatever it was, was sure to be hot!!

30

Reagan didn't tell Kennedy that she knew about Lucas's upcoming CD. If she had, Kennedy would know that Reagan was planning to put the moves on him, now that she knew that Lucas was a singer. So, she thought it best to play dumb, at least until they got to school.

Reagan had planned to corner Lucas in the courtyard, and chat him up, so that she could try and erase the way she had treated him, but by the time she got there, he and Kennedy were laughing it up, seemingly in their own world. Reagan retreated to her crew, and watched with the green eye of envy as Lucas teased with her sister, secretly wishing it was her instead.

"So, Rea," Madison moved closer to Reagan so the guys wouldn't hear their conversation, "have you thought some more about what I told you last night?" she asked, referring to their bathroom conversation.

"That's all I've been able to think about," she whispered, without taking her eyes off of Lucas. He was so cute, that she couldn't help staring. He no longer looked like a broke loser, but a rising star; and she wanted to go along for the ride, as he made it to the top. Reagan could picture herself cheesing for the paparazzi as they snapped Lucas's picture with her on his arm decked out in the latest designer dress. This was her big chance to be in the magazines that she worshiped.

"Have you come up with a plan yet?"

"A plan for what?" PG asked, sticking his nose where it didn't belong.

"Uh, this is an A and B conversation," Reagan said, pointing to herself and Madison, then said, "so C yourself out!"

PG was stunned at Reagan's rude remark, and looked shocked. He knew that Reagan had a sharp tongue, but she had never spoken to him so harshly, and he didn't know what to say.

"Oh, that's cold," Ian said, cracking up.

"Shut up, Ian, it's not that funny," PG shot back.

"Oh yeah, it is! You should see the look on your face. Your mouth is hanging down to your chin, and your eyes are bucked wide open, like somebody stuck your finger in a socket," Ian said, still in a fit of laughter.

"I take it you haven't looked in the mirror at your mug?" PG said, trying to make a comeback.

As the guys were trading insults, Reagan stepped closer to Madison and whispered, "Wait until our chemistry class, and watch me work." She then smiled a wicked grin.

"So, you're going to create some chemistry between

you and Lucas in chemistry? Aren't you the clever one?" Madison put her hand to her mouth and chuckled.

When the bell rang, Reagan stood back and watched as Lucas grabbed Kennedy's hand and they strolled inside the school as if they were on a date, strolling along the beach. *Enjoy him while you can, because he's going to be mine in a minute!* Reagan said, to herself.

Her first few classes went by at a snail's pace. Reagan barely paid attention to her teachers, because her mind was on Lucas. She still couldn't believe that he was a singer and rapper, and that he had a CD coming out in less than a week. Reagan's "Rich Radar" hadn't detected anything special about Lucas; otherwise, she would've been all over him, instead of treating him like he had cooties. Reagan wanted to kick herself for being so stupid! Lucas was the type of boy she was looking for— cute, and rich—to replace PG. With a recording contract, there was no doubt that Lucas could afford to keep her draped in jewelry and designer clothes. *I'm going to have to do some serious backpedaling*, Reagan thought, as she sat in her English class waiting for it to end.

When that class was finally over, she rushed down the hall to chemistry.

"Mad, come here," Reagan said, pulling Madison by the arm, before they walked into class.

"What's up?" Madison asked.

"I want you to get Kennedy's attention, so I can talk to Lucas alone. Okay?"

"Okay, but what am I supposed to talk to her about?

You know I'm probably the last person she wants to talk to," Madison told her.

"Make something up. Anything. I don't care. Just get her away from Lucas," Reagan said, sounding frantic.

"Okay, okay. Calm down."

Reagan poked her head through the classroom door and looked around. "Good; they're not in class yet. When they walk up, pull Kennedy to the side, and I'll take care of Lucas," she instructed.

"Got it," Madison said.

Then, as if on cue, Lucas and Kennedy walked up hand in hand.

"Hey, Kennedy!" Madison smiled.

"Hey, what's up?" Kennedy asked suspiciously.

"Can I talk to you for a second?"

"Why? Since when do you want to talk to me?" Kennedy said sarcastically.

"It won't take long; come here for a second," Madison said, stepping away from the door, indicating that she wanted Kennedy to follow her.

Kennedy looked at Lucas and said, "I'll be right back."

"Okay," he said, and let her hand go.

Kennedy walked to the side of the door where Madison was standing. "What do you want, Madison? Aren't you afraid that people will think that you're slumming, standing here talking to me?"

Madison didn't address her comment; she went right into her spiel. "Uh, I noticed those hot shoes that you've been rocking lately. You have such a good eye for fashion, and I was wondering if you ever thought about modeling?" Madison asked, coming up with a clever lie.

"Modeling? Me? What have you been smoking?" Kennedy asked, totally seeing through Madison's lie.

"I haven't been smoking anything. I was thinking that if you're interested, I could hook you up with my agent. They're always looking for new talent."

While Madison had Kennedy cornered, feeding her a load of bull, Reagan had followed Lucas inside the classroom, and was chatting him up.

"So, Lucas, how are you liking Walburton so far?" Reagan asked, making a lame attempt at small talk.

Lucas looked at her like she was growing another head out of the side of her neck. "What?"

"I said, how do you like Walburton?" she said again.

"Why do you care? And why are you rolling up in the Welcome Wagon now? If I remember correctly, you and your friends dissed me in the courtyard on my first day," he told her without mincing words.

"We were not dissing you. I think you misunderstood," she said, acting like he was mistaken. "Anyway, I was wondering if you're finding your way around campus okay. If not, I can show you around," she offered, refusing to be thrown off by his comment.

"I'm thinking uh…NO!" he said, nearly shouting.

"Okay, since you're all settled in, why don't we meet after school and I can show you some cool places to hang out," Reagan said, still refusing to ease up.

"That would again be a NO!"

As Lucas was shooting Reagan down faster than a skeet shooter, Kennedy walked up.

"No to what?" Kennedy asked, staring directly at her sister.

Lucas put his arm around her shoulder, making it clear that he was with Kennedy. "Your sister wants to be my tour guide, but I told her no," he said, point-blank.

Kennedy rolled her eyes at Reagan. "I'll bet she wants to be more than your tour guide."

"Whatever!" Reagan said, flipped her hair and walked to her seat.

Lucas can act funky if he wants to. He knows that he wants me. He's trying to play hard to get. It may take longer than I thought to get him away from Kennedy, but I'm not stopping until I'm his girlfriend, and everyone in the world knows it! Reagan thought, as she slammed open her textbook, and waited for class to start.

31

"I'll pick you up at seven-fifteen," Lucas told Kennedy as they were leaving school.

"Okay. I'll be ready!" she said, smiling. Kennedy was so excited to be going with Lucas to his launch party that she felt like skipping down the street, but that would've been too juvenile, so she walked beside him like the mature teenager that she was.

"Good, 'cause I hate to wait. Most chicks are sooo slow," he said, emphasizing the word "so."

Kennedy pushed him against the shoulder. "Boy, here you go with that 'most chicks' stuff. You *must* have a metal plate in your head—either that or you need to take the short bus to school! I keep telling you the same thing over, and over, and over! I'M NOT LIKE MOST GIRLS!!" she shouted.

Lucas broke out laughing. "I love to get you all riled up; it's so funny, the way you overreact!"

She smacked his shoulder again. "Glad I could give you a good laugh this afternoon," she said sarcastically.

"Aw, come on, Kennedy, don't get all sensitive on me.

I'm only teasing." He put his arm around her shoulder. "Come on. I'll walk you home."

"Thanks, but I'm not going home," she said, still a little ticked off.

"Where are you going?" he asked possessively.

"Noneya."

"What?"

"None of your business," she said, laughing.

"Ha, ha."

"It's not so funny, when somebody else gets to laugh at your expense, now is it?" she asked.

"Touché. Anyway, Ms. Smarty, I'll see you later," he said, then slowed his pace, leaned in and kissed her on the cheek.

Kennedy stopped dead in her tracks, and put her hand to her cheek. She couldn't believe that Lucas had kissed her. It was their first kiss, and in public no less. Kennedy stood there on the sidewalk in shock. She felt as if she were in a fairytale, and the handsome prince had given her the kiss of life! Lucas didn't see her gesture, since he kept walking.

"Come on, Girl. What are you doing standing there?" he asked, finally realizing that Kennedy wasn't beside him anymore.

"Uh…you kissed me," she said, finding her voice.

"Yeah, so? Why? You didn't want me to?" he asked, sounding as if it were no big deal.

"No, I didn't mind. It took me by surprise, that's all," she said, walking toward him.

Lucas placed his hands on her shoulders. "Look, Kennedy, I don't want to play any games with you. I'm digging you. I mean, you're mad cool, and I like hanging out with you. And I was thinking…uh…that we should be exclusive? Whatcha think?"

Kennedy looked to the side of her, and then in back of her. She felt like she was getting punked, and at any moment Ashton Kutcher was going to come running up with a camera crew, and say, "You've been Punk'd!"

Lucas saw the surprised look on her face. "I'm sure this seems like it's coming out of left field, but I've been thinking about it a lot, and being a couple makes sense to me. I know we only met a few weeks ago, but I think we really click, don't you?"

"Yeah, we definitely click. I'm just surprised that you want to get into a relationship, especially since you're getting ready to blow up," she said, getting to the point.

"I know the timing seems off, but to be honest, I never really had a serious girlfriend and like I said, I like hanging out with you. Besides, once those groupies start stalking me, it would be nice to know that I got my girl and don't need to be bothered with them skanks who only want me 'cuz I'm famous."

Kennedy blushed when he said, "my girl." "It's funny, most guys would be the opposite, and want to date a million and two girls, but…"

Lucas cut her off. "Excuse me, but I'm not like most guys," he said, using her line.

"Touché!"

"So, what's it gonna be? You wanna be my girl or what?"

"Yes, I wanna be your girl," she answered in a small, shy voice.

"Good." He kissed her on the cheek again, grabbed her hand, and started walking. "So...now that you're my girl, you gonna tell me where you're going?"

"We haven't been dating two minutes, and you're clocking me already!" Kennedy said, smiling.

"Come on, woman, tell me," he said, putting his arm around her shoulders.

"Okay, boyfriend, if you must know, I'm going to get a new outfit for tonight."

"Just like a chick to go shopping a few hours before a party."

"What does it matter, so long as I look fly!" She smiled.

"Just don't be late."

"I won't. I'm going to hop on the train now," she said, as they approached the subway station. "I'll see you tonight."

"Seven-fifteen, and don't be late," he said again.

"I won't be," she said, as she trotted down the stairs.

On the way to Barneys, Kennedy replayed the scene with Lucas over and over in her mind. He had actually asked her to be his girlfriend, and she couldn't believe it. Most guys shied away from commitment like it was a life sentence on Rikers Island, but Lucas was embracing it. He definitely wasn't like other boys. He was one of a kind!

The train ride was short, and in no time, she was at Barneys. Kennedy wasn't familiar with the layout of the store, since she rarely shopped there, but tonight was a special occasion, so she decided to spend the big bucks, and buy a designer outfit. She stopped a passing sales-person to ask for directions.

"Excuse me, Miss, can you tell me where the designer clothes are?"

The salesperson pointed toward the escalators, and told Kennedy to go upstairs. "There are women's designer collections on two, three, four and five," she said, with an air of someone who knew the store like the back of her hand.

"Thanks," Kennedy said, and made her way to the escalators.

She stepped off the moving stairs when a cobalt-blue dress that a mannequin was wearing caught her eye. She fingered the silk material. *This is too thin. I'll probably rip it before the night is over*, Kennedy thought, and then walked further onto the sales floor, and began browsing.

"Hey, Peggy, isn't that that little rich brat that was in here a while ago?"

Peggy squinted her eyes in Kennedy's direction. "Looks like her."

"Where's her snotty friend with the Marc Jacobs purse?" Norelle asked, still remembering the new purse that hung off Madison's shoulder.

"Probably downstairs buying another eighteen-hundred-dollar bag. Kids these days don't have any sense of value. Or should I say these rich kids don't have any sense of what a dollar is worth. That's why I'm always preaching to Lucas not to waste his money on material things that will depreciate in a matter of months," Peggy said.

"You're right. The girls who come in here spend a thousand dollars like it's nothing. I'm so glad that you've grounded Lucas in reality."

"Thanks. I'm trying," Peggy said.

"You want me to handle this little brat?" Norelle asked.

"No, I got her number now. If little Ms. Thing thinks she's going to be rude to me this time, she better think again. Besides, she'll be my last customer of the day. I'm leaving early, so I won't be late for Lucas's release party. You're still coming tonight, right?"

"Of course. I wouldn't miss it. I'll be there around nine."

"Good. At least I won't be the only overgrown adult there." Peggy laughed, then headed in Kennedy's direction.

"Hello, may I help you?"

Kennedy turned around, and smiled. "Hi. I'm looking for this in a size six," she said, holding up a Lia Kes dress with a geometric dot pattern.

Peggy was taken aback. The last time the girl was in the store, she didn't even speak, and nearly shoved a dress in Peggy's arms. "We should have a six, around here somewhere," Peggy said, looking through the dresses on the rack. "Oh, here's a six," she said, taking the dress off the rack. "Would you like for me to start a fitting room for you?"

"Yes, please; that would be great."

Wow, what a shift in personality. She must be bipolar, Peggy thought. "No problem," Peggy said, and walked back to the dressing rooms.

Kennedy found two more dresses, and walked over to where Peggy stood. "I'd also like to try these on."

"Sure thing; are you ready now?"

"Yes, if I can't decide from these three, then it's hopeless," she said with a smile.

"Don't say that. I'm sure one of these dresses will look good on you." Peggy showed Kennedy the dressing room, and went back to the counter.

"So, how's it going with little Ms. Diva?" Norelle asked.

"Surprisingly, she's not being a bitch this time. She's actually quite pleasant."

"Now I find that hard to believe."

"It's true. Maybe someone knocked her down a few pegs."

As they were sizing her up, Kennedy came out of the fitting room. "I'll take this one," she said, holding up the Lia Kes dress.

"Great choice. Will you be paying cash or will it be a charge?" Peggy asked.

"I'll be paying with my debit card. I hate charging stuff," Kennedy said, handing over the card. Unlike in the shoe store Kennedy wasn't experiencing sticker shock this time, she knew that Barneys was expensive, so she didn't cringe at the price tag. Besides, it wasn't like she spent hundreds of dollars on a dress every day.

"Smart girl!" Peggy said, before she knew it.

Kennedy blushed. "Thanks."

Once her dress was wrapped up and paid for, Kennedy headed home to shower and change for the night of her life!

32

Reagan happened to be looking out of her bedroom window as Kennedy was strolling down the street. From what Reagan could tell, it looked like Kennedy was in a happy mood, she was walking casually like she didn't have a care in the world, and seemed to be whistling. Seeing her sister walking toward home wasn't a big deal, but what Kennedy carried with her was! In her hand was a black shopping bag; not just any black bag, but a bag from BARNEYS! She could spot the Barneys bag with the silver lettering anywhere. Reagan was in shock. Kennedy had never expressed any interest in shopping. Except as of late, now she was shopping at Barneys, Reagan's favorite store. As a matter of fact, Kennedy had always ridiculed Reagan and Madison for spending too much money on clothes, and here she was apparently doing the same thing!

"What the hell is she doing shopping at MY store?!" Reagan hissed under her breath.

Reagan thought about bum-rushing her sister at the front door, and asking point blank what was in the bag, but she knew that Kennedy would give her a smart-ass answer, and she wasn't in the mood for a verbal sparring match, especially after having been dissed by Lucas. Reagan was determined to find out what Kennedy had bought, but she had a better plan, than just straight-up asking.

Reagan waited until she heard the shower running in Kennedy's bathroom, and then crept into her sister's bedroom. She didn't have to look far to satisfy her curiosity. There, lying on one of the twin beds, was a gorgeous, colorful, geometric print dress. Reagan walked closer to get a better look. She immediately looked inside at the label.

"Lia Kes!" she said, under her breath. Lia Kes was a relatively new designer, and her clothes were hot!

How the hell does Kennedy know about Lia Kes? If she's paying top dollar for a designer dress, then she must be going someplace special, she thought. Reagan fingered the expensive material, as she pondered the situation. Then it occurred to her. *I'll bet Kennedy's going to Lucas's CD release party!*

With that thought in mind, Reagan bolted out of Kennedy's room, and made a dash into her own. She immediately went to the phone and called Madison.

"Hey, Rea, what's up? I can't talk long, I'm getting dressed for Lucas's release party," Madison said, all in one breath the second she picked up.

"That's why I'm calling. I think Kennedy is going to the party with Lucas," she blurted out.

"What makes you think that?"

"I just came out of her room, and guess what I saw?!" she asked, sounding like she had spotted the Loch Ness monster.

"What? What did you see?" Madison asked, totally intrigued.

"A dress."

"A dress? Is that all? I thought you were going to say you saw something juicy like a box of condoms and a *Playgirl* magazine."

"No, no, you don't get it. This wasn't an ordinary dress; it was a Lia Kes!"

"What?? Are you shitting me? Her dresses are the bomb! And not too many people know about her yet. What the hell is Kennedy doing with a designer dress like that?" Madison asked, now totally getting the point.

"That's what I've been trying to tell you. Why else would she be shopping at Barneys? Personally, I didn't think she knew where the store was. She obviously bought it to wear tonight!"

"Yeah, that does make sense, especially since Kennedy couldn't care less about designer stuff. So, what are you going to do? Are you going to 'accidentally' spill some fingernail polish remover, or smear some make-up on it?"

"No, that would be too obvious and, she would know that it was me. Besides, it wouldn't stop her from going to the party. Knowing Kennedy, she'd probably pick some ghastly thing out of her closet, and go anyway.

What I need is my own invitation, so I can cozy up to Lucas, and try again to get him interested in me. Do you think your agent can get me in tonight?" Reagan asked.

"I wish, Rea, but I doubt it. These types of events are so hard to get into that if you're not on somebody's A list, then you can forget about getting past the velvet ropes," Madison told her.

"Damn! Damn! Damn!" Reagan hissed, stomping her foot on the carpeted floor.

"There's always Monday. You can try and corner him again in chemistry class, and maybe this time you'll have more luck," Madison said, trying to come up with another plan of attack.

"No. That's not good enough. I can't wait until Monday, besides I need more than a few seconds before class starts to work my magic. I need a party like tonight with a lot of people around, so that I can distract him without Kennedy looking over my shoulder."

"That definitely sounds like a good plan, and I wish I could dig up an invite for you, but like I said, there's no way my agent will be able to get you in," Madison said, nearly apologizing.

"That's okay. I know you would hook me up if you could. Let me think about this for a second," Reagan said, getting quiet. Then a few moments later, she blurted out, "Oh, I got it! I got it!"

"What? What are you going to do?" Madison asked,

wanting to know what type of devious scheme Reagan had conjured up.

"I don't have time to explain now. Be sure to keep your cell on vibrate, and expect a call from me later tonight," Reagan said, mysteriously.

"Okay."

"Look, I gotta make a run before it's too late. Don't forget, keep your phone close," and with that, Reagan hung up.

She grabbed her purse, and house keys, and bolted out of the front door. If her scheme worked according to plan, she would not only be at the release party, but Lucas's new girlfriend before the night was over!

33

Kennedy stood in the mirror putting on mascara, trying not to poke out her eye. She wasn't experienced in the art of make-up, but thought that tonight instead of only wearing lip gloss, she'd step up her game with some blush, eyeliner and mascara. Kennedy wanted to look extra special, in case her picture was snapped by the paparazzi. She looked at herself in the mirror, and thought that she had come a long way in a matter of weeks. Since meeting Lucas, Kennedy had made adjustments to her hair, and wardrobe. She'd even given up wearing her old beat-up Army jacket every day. If someone had told Kennedy that she would be buying clothes at Barneys a month ago, she probably would've laughed in their face. Kennedy was always ragging on Reagan and Madison for overspending, and now she was doing the same thing. It wasn't exactly the same thing, since she didn't plan on making a habit out of wasting money every day on designer clothes. She still cared about saving the environment, ending famine, and world peace. But Kennedy had to admit—even if it was only to herself—that she enjoyed wearing pretty clothes, and styling her hair differently.

Maybe I was too harsh on Reagan and Madison, she thought as she looked in the mirror, then thought again, *Nah, I wasn't too hard on them. I may have changed my style a little bit, but I'm nowhere near as selfish and conceited as they are. All they care about is boys and clothes.*

After painstakingly coating her lashes, Kennedy dotted her lips with gloss, combed her hair, which she had straightened earlier, and spritzed her neck with some perfume borrowed from her mother. She went back into her room, slipped on the dress and a pair of heels. Kennedy glanced over at the clock on her nightstand. It was seven-o-five. Ten more minutes, and Lucas would be downstairs. She felt like Cinderella awaiting her "Golden Carriage." Although, she still had a few minutes to kill, Kennedy gathered her clutch purse, and headed downstairs.

Kennedy waited in the foyer, and looked out of the beveled glass door so that she could see when Lucas pulled up. He hadn't told her what type of car he'd be in; he just said that he'd be "styling." Styling could mean anything from a stretch Hummer, to a Benz, to a Bentley, so she didn't know exactly what to expect.

As she was waiting, and watching, her cell phone rang. Kennedy looked at the caller ID, and it was Lucas calling.

"Hey, I'm pulling up in front in two minutes," he said, when she answered the phone.

"Okay, I'm already downstairs," she said, and hit the end button.

Kennedy stepped out of her gray stone building, locked the door behind her, and when she turned back around, she gasped. Pulling up curbside was a glossy black Mercedes Maybach! Ian's father had a Maybach. She'd seen it several times in front of Walburton, when the driver picked up Ian and his crew. Of course, Kennedy had never been offered a ride, and never desired to see the inside of the luxury car until now. As she walked toward the car, the driver got out, walked swiftly around to the passenger side, and opened the door for her. *Wow, I feel so special*, she thought, with a huge smile spreading across her face.

"Hey, there!" Lucas said the minute the door opened.

Kennedy slid into the back seat, and was surprised to see other people in the car; she had assumed that she and Lucas were riding in the car alone. She looked around at the faces, and smiled.

"Kennedy, this is my mother, Mrs. Lucas, and this is my manager, Kevin Myers. Mom, and Kevin, this is Kennedy," he said, making introductions all around.

"Hi." Kennedy smiled.

Looking at Kennedy, Peggy said, without skipping a beat, "I know you. You were in Barneys this afternoon."

"I remember you too!" Kennedy said, recognizing the face of the saleswoman who had helped her earlier that day.

"That dress looks great on you," Peggy commented.

"Thanks!" Kennedy beamed.

"What a small world, when Lucas said that he was picking up a friend from school, I had no idea that it would be one of my customers," Peggy told her.

"Yes, it is a small world. You never know who you're going to meet; that's why it's nice to be nice," Kennedy said, sounding older than her teenage years.

"It's funny that you say that, because the first time I waited on you, you were anything but nice," Peggy said, with a straight face.

Kennedy looked at her like she was craxy with an "X." "Excuse me?"

Peggy stared directly at Kennedy. "You don't remember the time when you came in with your friend? You guys were buying up the store, and acting like little princesses."

"No, it wasn't me. Today was the first time that I've ever shopped at Barneys."

Shaking her head up and down, Peggy contradicted Kennedy, "Yes, it was you alright."

"Wait a minute; did you say that I was with another girl?"

"Yes, she was tall, with flaming red hair."

"No, Ma'am, that wasn't me; it was my sister, Reagan, and her best friend, Madison."

"See, Ma, Kennedy has a twin sister, and they are identical," Lucas said, jumping into their conversation.

"How nice it must be to have a twin, I bet you guys are thicker than thieves," Kevin commented, also joining the conversation.

"No, man, you couldn't be more wrong. Kennedy and Reagan are total opposites. Reagan and her crew are straight-up snobs. They dissed me on my first day, but now that they know I'm getting ready to blow up, they wanna be friends," Lucas said.

"Didn't I tell you things like that were going to happen? And wait until you're in all the teen magazines, and on television, more and more groupies are going to surface," Kevin said.

"Don't worry. I can handle myself. I've been taught by the best," Lucas said, kissing his mom on the cheek.

"That's right. I raised a smart kid!"

"Not to change the subject, but we're almost there, and I need to tell you a few things, Lucas," Kevin interrupted.

"Yeah, man?"

"When we get to the party, there's going to be press waiting outside. You'll give interviews to BET, VH1, MTV, and a few magazines. Give brief answers to avoid talking too much. Remember, less is more. You don't want these reporters twisting your words."

"Okay. Got it."

"And, ladies, while Lucas is on the red carpet giving interviews, I want you to go inside straight to the VIP area," Kevin said, now turning his attention to Peggy and Kennedy.

"How will we know where the VIP area is located?" Peggy asked.

"Because your names are on the list, and there will be

a guard at the front door checking names. Once you're cleared, a hostess will escort you to VIP."

"Oh, okay. Now my friend Norelle is coming, and so is Lucas's friend Devin. Will they also be on the list?" Peggy asked.

"Of course; all of Lucas's people have been cleared."

"Excellent. Oh, I'm so excited! This will be my first time walking down a red carpet!" Peggy exclaimed.

"Mine, too," Kennedy chimed in.

"Your first, but not your last. Peggy, your son is going places," Kevin beamed.

No sooner had Kevin given them the briefing than the car was pulling up in front of the SoHo Grand hotel where the party was taking place.

"Wow, look at all those reporters," Kennedy said, peering out of the window at the waiting press.

"Everybody wants to get the scoop on this rising star! Are we ready?" Kevin asked.

They all nodded their heads, and said, "Yes."

"Okay, ladies, you go first, and Lucas and I will follow shortly," Kevin instructed.

The driver came around and opened the door for them, and Peggy and Kennedy got out. Since they were 'nobodies' in the eyes of the press, no one stopped them as they made their way to the door.

"Come on, Lucas," Kevin said, getting out of the back seat.

The moment the reporters saw Lucas emerge from

the car, flashbulbs started popping, and they began yelling his name. "Lucas, over here... This way, Lucas... Lucas Williams, how 'bout an interview?!"

Lucas stopped and beamed a two-hundred-watt smile, as his picture was being taken. He was pumped with adrenaline, and being on the red carpet felt surreal! He'd seen some of his idols do interviews on television, and now it was his turn to shine.

Kevin nudged his arm, indicating that the photo-op with that particular photographer was over. He then led Lucas over to a waiting reporter.

"Lucas, I listened to your CD, and it's the bomb. Every song is hot."

"Thanks." Lucas smiled.

"Do you have any plans to collaborate with Jay-Z, Dr. Dre or Jermaine Dupri?"

"No, not right now," Lucas said, short and sweet like Kevin had told him.

"What about doing a remix on your new single?"

"No remixes yet."

"Are you working on your next album?"

"No, not yet."

"Sorry, but we need to make the rounds," Kevin interrupted.

"Good luck with your career," the reporter said.

"Thanks, man," Lucas responded.

Lucas did a few more interviews, before he and Kevin began to make their way inside. As he was walking toward the entrance, he heard a reporter yelling out someone else's name.

"Madison Reynolds, over here!"

Lucas swung around, and sure enough it was the red-head from school striking a pose on the red carpet. *What the hell is she doing here?* he thought, and then disappeared inside.

34

"Madison, Madison, over here!" yelled a tabloid reporter. "You look awesome! Who are you wearing?" he asked, commenting on Madison's emerald-green, empire-waisted silk dress.

She flashed her professional model smile, and then said, "It's one of a kind by Issey Miyake."

"Madison, just a few questions!" another reported yelled from behind the ropes. "Are you here as Lucas's date?"

"She's too young to date," her grandmother answered.

Why can't Nancy mind her own business? She's making me seem like a two-year-old! Madison fumed to herself.

"If you're not here as his date, then are you guys friends?" the reporter asked, pressing the issue.

"Sure they're friends. They go to the same school," Nancy said, answering again.

"Come on, Nancy, let's go inside," Madison whispered to her grandmother, eager to end the Q and A.

"Of course, dear," Nancy said, leading the way into the party.

As Madison was making her way inside, she felt her

cell phone buzzing inside of her purse. She wanted to answer, but knew that Nancy would have a gazillion questions, and she didn't want to be grilled.

"Your names, please?" demanded the beefy keeper of the gate.

"Renée and Madison Reynolds," Nancy said, continuing to speak for Madison.

The doorman flipped through the pages of the guest list until he found their names. "Go right in; the VIP hostess will seat you," he said, in a deadpan voice.

Madison adjusted her long hair behind her left ear, and walked ahead of Nancy, trying to put some distance between them. The music was pumping and people were everywhere. She looked around and spotted a few models that she knew, drinking at the bar. *What I wouldn't give for an ice-cold martini*, she thought.

"Why do they have to play the music so loud?" Nancy asked, catching up to her granddaughter.

Because it's a party for young people, and you should be at home knitting a sweater or baking cookies, like most grandmothers!

"Nancy, if it's too noisy for you, why don't you go home? I'll be all right by myself," Madison suggested, trying to get rid of her grandmother.

"Dear, I wouldn't dream of leaving you here alone. Come on, let's get some cranberry juice," Nancy said, walking toward the bar.

Only if I can have a double shot of vodka in it! As Madison was dreaming of a cocktail, she felt her phone buzz again. "Nancy, I have to go to the ladies' room, I'll be right back," she said, rushing away before Nancy had a chance to follow.

Once inside the restroom, Madison hit the speed dial to Reagan.

"I've been calling you. Why didn't you pick up?" Reagan asked, in a huff.

"Because Nancy's been breathing down my neck, and I haven't had a second alone."

"Have you seen Lucas yet?"

"Yeah, I saw him on the red carpet."

"How did he look?"

"Good, like a cross between Mario, Justin Timberlake and Chris Brown, all rolled into one! He has on a European-cut black shirt, and a pair of snug black pants. He looks totally different out of that baggy uniform. I can't believe that we screwed the pooch on this one. We treated him like shit, when he's going to be a mega-star!" Madison said.

"Don't worry, Mad, once I win him over, he'll forget how we acted. Trust me," Reagan said, confidently.

"I hope you're right. Since Lucas and I are both in the entertainment industry, it'd be great if we were friends instead of rivals."

"I agree; that's why you have to sneak me into the party!"

"And how am I supposed to do that? There's an Incredible Hulk type guarding the guest list."

"There's gotta be a back door that nobody is watching.

I can get in that way," Reagan said, refusing to be deterred.

"Good idea! I'll find the back door and call you back."

"Hurry. I'm getting ready to hop in a taxi, and should be there soon."

"Okay," Madison said, and clicked off her phone.

Madison poked her head out of the ladies' room, making sure that Nancy didn't see her come out. Luckily, her grandmother was nowhere in sight. Madison mingled through the crowd until she made her way to the rear of the hotel. "Bingo!" she said, the instant she spotted the service entrance. She took out her phone, and quickly dialed Reagan to tell her the good news!

35

The lighting in the room was dim, giving the party a hip, grown-up vibe. The event was in full swing with guests mingling, drinking and swaying to the music. The crowd was an eclectic mix of entertainment execs, entertainers, both old school and new school, a few high-profile heiresses and their entourages. Posters of Lucas's album cover were hung on the walls, and complimentary copies of his CD were being passed out by models dressed like the dancers in his video.

"Man, this party is off da heezy fo sheezy!" Devin exclaimed as he surveyed the room with his eyes bucked wide staring at the various celebrities. "Hey, isn't that Rihanna?" Devin asked, practically drooling.

Lucas casually scanned the crowd, and spotted the hot young singer. "Yeah, that's her," he said nonchalantly.

"Man, why you sounding so dry? Rihanna is PHINE!!!"

"Yeah, she is, but my girl is just as fine," Lucas said, giving kudos to both the star and his girlfriend.

"I gotta admit Kennedy does look tight tonight. She got any friends?" Devin asked, forever the hound dog.

"Man, she doesn't have any friends that'll be interested in a dawg like you," Lucas said, teasing his friend. "Come on, let's get back to VIP. I'm sure everyone's wondering where we've been." Devin had begged Lucas to walk the party with him, so that he could get his mack on, but of course none of the A-Listers were interested in engaging a pedestrian.

"So, you singing tonight?" Devin asked, as they cut through the crowd.

"Yeah, there's a small stage set up in one of the other rooms."

"Are the dancers gonna be on stage with you?" Devin asked, remembering the hot girl he had lusted after at the video shoot.

"No, it'll just be me on stage. Kevin wants to showcase another song from the album, so I won't be singing the song from the video."

"What song are you singing? Have I heard it before?"

"It's a love song, and no, you've never heard it. We put the finishing touches on it a few weeks ago. It's dope. I think you'll like it."

"I know I will." Devin tugged Lucas's arm to stop him from walking, and then said, "Man, I never told you this before, but you can sing your ass off! I know we boys now, but once you're a mega-star, I hope you don't forget your homie," Devin said, sounding sincere.

Lucas grabbed Devin in a headlock. "Awe, man, don't get all soft on a brother. You know we'll always be boys, no matter how many records I sell."

"I ain't soft," Devin said, squirming his way out of the

headlock. "I'm a playa," he announced, finally breaking loose.

"Come on, Playa, let's get back to VIP." Lucas turned to walk away, but turned back. "Devin, thanks for the compliment. I really appreciate it."

"Now who's getting soft?"

"Shut up!" Lucas said in jest, poking Devin in the arm.

A few minutes later, the boys were entering the private VIP area where waiters were passing out munchies, glasses of champagne, and sparkling cider for the under-aged guests.

"Hey, Aunt Norelle," Lucas said, leaning over and kissing his play-aunt on the cheek. "When did you get here?"

"A little while ago. I worked the late shift tonight. Look at you, looking all grown up," she said, giving him an appraising once-over.

"Thanks. Did you meet Kennedy?"

"Yes, and at first I thought that she was that little brat from Barneys, but your mother filled me in about her having a wicked twin sister. All I can say is that I'm sure glad you're not dating the bratty one," Norelle said, totally speaking her mind.

"Naw, Aunt Norelle, you know I'm too down to be dating a snob. Now let me go see about my girl," Lucas said, walking away to find Kennedy.

Kennedy was standing near the back of the room, bopping her head to the beat, when Lucas walked up.

"Yo, Ken, are you having a good time?" Lucas asked.

"Yeah, this is a really nice party. Thanks for inviting me." She smiled.

"Who else would I bring?"

"I could think of about a gazillion girls, who would love to be here with you."

"Hey, speaking of girls, guess who's here?"

Kennedy's heart skipped a beat. She was hoping that he wasn't going to say Reagan. Although she knew that her sister didn't have an invitation, Kennedy wouldn't put it past Reagan to crash the party. *Wait, wait a minute, this is a private party with a tight guest list, so there's no way Reagan can get in*, she thought, calming herself down. "Who did you see?" she finally asked.

"That redheaded chick from school!"

Kennedy's calmness quickly disappeared. If Madison was at the party, then Reagan couldn't be far behind. "You mean Madison?" she asked, knowing exactly who Lucas was talking about, but she asked just the same, in case there was another redheaded girl at Walburton whom she hadn't seen before.

"I guess that's her name. She's always with your sister."

"Yeah, that's Madison alright. Was she by herself?" Kennedy asked, praying that Reagan wasn't tagging along. Suddenly, the memory of Reagan taking her boyfriend years ago came rushing back, and Kennedy went into panic mode. She was crazy about Lucas, and didn't want to lose him to her sister.

"No, she wasn't by herself. She was with some old chick."

"Really? I wonder who that is."

"I don't know, but whoever it was was talking to the reporters, while Madison posed for the cameras."

"Maybe it was her agent."

"Agent?" Lucas asked, with his nose twisted up.

"Yeah; she's a model."

"Oh, that's probably why she's here. I'm sure the PR person sent invites to the hot models around town."

"Sooo...you think she's hot?" Kennedy asked, with her hand on her hip.

He pulled her close to him. "Not as hot as you!"

"Hey, guys!"

They took their attention off of each other, and focused on the person in front of them. "Hi," they both said, in a dry, deadpan tone.

"What's up?!" she asked, flashing all of her bright-white teeth.

Lucas and Kennedy didn't answer; they stood there on mute, and looked at her like she had just landed from Pluto.

"Lucas, congratulations on your CD. When my agent set up a personal appearance, I had no idea that it was for you! What a small world!" Madison said, talking fast, trying to get a response from Lucas.

"Perfect, just the two people I was looking for!" said a photographer walking up to them. "Come on; let me get a few shots of you two."

Lucas grabbed Kennedy around the waist. "Sure, go ahead."

"Uh…I was talking about you and Madison Reynolds. The singer and the supermodel," he said, pushing them together, and nudging Kennedy to the side. "Come on, Lucas; put your arm around her," he directed, and began snapping away.

Lucas put up his hand. "Yo, man. Stop."

"Just a few more." *Snap. Snap. Snap.*

"Yo, man. I said, stop! I'm not taking any pictures with her; now delete those pictures," Lucas demanded.

"Come on, Lucas; let's take some publicity shots. It'll be good for the both of us," Madison whispered underneath her breath so the photographer couldn't hear.

"Girl, I ain't trying to take no pictures with you!" Lucas said, raising his voice, and walking over to Kennedy, leaving Madison standing by herself.

As Lucas was dissing Madison, her cell phone rang. She looked at the caller ID. It was Reagan. "That's okay about the pictures. I gotta go," she said, and walked away.

"Can you believe her? A few weeks ago, she assumed I was a poor scholarship student, and now that she knows about my CD, she wants to cozy up to me!"

"Calm down. Don't let her ruin your big night," Kennedy said.

"Come on, Lucas, it's time for you to get ready to perform," Kevin said, walking up to them.

"Okay, I'll be right there." Lucas then turned to Kennedy. "Sorry about that rude photographer. He shouldn't have pushed you aside like that."

"Don't worry about it, Lucas. At least you made yourself clear to Madison. I don't think she'll be bugging you again about any more photo-ops."

"Yeah, you're right. Come on. I'll walk you over to the stage," he said, grabbing her by the hand.

Kennedy found a spot right in the front along with Lucas's mom, and her friend. After standing there for about five minutes, the lights in the room dimmed, and the music started playing. The stage lights turned blue, and out came Lucas. He had changed his clothes from all black into an all-white outfit.

Lucas strolled to the middle of the stage, grabbed the microphone off the stand, and started singing.

"Girl, the first time I laid eyes on you, I knew you were the one for me," he sang, staring directly at his girlfriend.

Kennedy couldn't believe that Lucas was actually singing to her. Even though the room was crowded with people, she felt as if it were only her and Lucas in the room.

"Girl, will you be my queen? Will you help me fulfill my dreams?" he sang.

Kennedy was all smiles as Lucas sang, and when the song was over, she fought through the crowd to make her way backstage to give him a big juicy kiss to thank him for the song.

"So, how did you like the song?" Lucas asked the moment he saw her standing near the rear of the stage.

"It was so romantic." She walked over, wrapped her arms around his neck, and began tonguing him. She pulled him in closer and pressed her body tightly against his.

Lucas's hormones kicked in and he totally forgot where they were. He grabbed her around the waist, and began kissing her harder.

"What the hell?!" a voice from behind yelled.

Lucas looked at Kennedy, and his mouth fell open.

"Why'd you stop?"

"Get the hell away from me, girl!" he yelled at Reagan who was dressed exactly like Kennedy. She had on the same dress, and her hair was styled identically to her sister's.

"Come on, Lucas, I know you were feeling it," Reagan said, ignoring Kennedy.

Kennedy walked up and pushed her sister aside. "Get lost, Reagan. Your little plan of trying to impersonate me didn't work."

"Oh, yes, it did. I'll bet he's never kissed you like he just kissed me," Reagan said, standing there with her hand on her hip.

Lucas looked from one sister to the other. He could hardly tell them apart. The only discerning factor was Reagan's foul attitude. "Look, girl, I only kissed you because I thought that you were Kennedy."

"Kennedy wished that she could kiss like that. Lucas, I hate to tell you, but you picked the wrong sister. Kennedy is too much of a nerd to know what a man like you needs."

Lucas looked at Reagan and shook his head. "You're pathetic. How can you stand there and diss your own sister like that?" he asked, coming to Kennedy's defense.

"It's okay, Lucas; she can't help herself. Reagan is all about Reagan, and only cares about someone if they can benefit her. Trust me; she wouldn't be all about you if you were not a singer."

"Yeah, I know. Come on, Kennedy, let's get out of here. This place is full of pests," he said, giving Reagan the evil eye. Lucas put his arm around Kennedy and the two of them walked away, leaving Reagan standing there looking stupid!

36

"**S**o what happened after I let you through the service entrance?" Madison asked Reagan. It was Saturday morning, and this was the first chance they had had to discuss what happened the night before. "Once I opened the door you bolted through like lightning, and ran so fast that I couldn't keep up, with those heels I had on."

"I heard Lucas singing, and followed the music. I found the entry to the backstage area, and decided to wait for him there until he finished."

"What'd you do once the song was over?"

"I really didn't have to do much. The second he saw me waiting backstage, he automatically assumed that I was Kennedy. He…"

Madison cut her off, "Rea, dressing like your sister was brilliant. How did you pull that one off?"

"I told you that I saw her outfit when she was in the shower, so after I hung up from talking to you, I left the house, jumped in a taxi and went straight to Barneys. Luckily there was another Lia Kes dress in my size, so I bought it, and then went home to transform myself into Kennedy. It was so easy. Since we are physically identical, all I had to do was make a few adjustments to my hair, and with the same outfit on, not even you would've been able to tell us apart," Reagan explained.

"Yeah, I know. If I didn't know better, I would have thought that I was letting Kennedy into the party instead of you. Okay, so tell me what happened once the song was over," Madison asked again.

"He asked how I liked his song. I told him that it was romantic, and then I went over, wrapped my arms around his neck, and gave him a big, juicy kiss!"

"OMIGOD!! No, you didn't!"

"Oh, yes, I did!"

"How was it? Can he kiss?" Madison wanted to know.

"Yes, he can kiss his butt off, and everything was going according to my plan until Kennedy busted us."

"OMIGOD!" Madison shrieked again. "What did you do then?"

"I tried to persuade Lucas that I was the better choice, and that he had picked the wrong sister. I even said that I know what a man like him needs, and…"

"Wait a minute, why'd you say that? You're still a virgin, so how can you know that much about sex?"

"What's there to know? It's not rocket science. It's all about chemistry, and following your instincts. The way Lucas was holding onto me, while we were kissing, I know that he was feeling me, like I was feeling him. I think that if you're really vibing with someone that strongly, then it'll translate into good sex," Reagan said confidently, like she was an old pro.

"Yeah, I guess you have a point. Anyway, what'd he say, once you told him that?"

"He said something lame, and I wasn't about to stand there and listen to his rhetoric, so I flipped my hair to the side, and strutted off like a true diva," Reagan lied, embarrassed to tell Madison that Lucas had dissed her and walked away with his arm around Kennedy.

"Good for you. Why be into somebody who's not into you? Besides, PG is still crazy about you, and as long as he keeps showering you with gifts du jour, I'm sure you can continue to put up with him."

"You bet I can. I don't plan on letting PG and his presents go anytime soon."

"Hold on; someone's calling," Madison said, hearing the call-waiting beep.

"Okay."

A minute later, she clicked back over to Reagan. "That was Ian. He wants me to come over this afternoon. He's home alone and wants some company."

"Why don't I call PG and the four of us can have some fun?"

"No, Rea, not that type of company. Ian wants a private party with the two of us," Madison whispered into the receiver.

"OH! I get it! Sooo...you gonna give him some this time?"

"I think so. All this talk about chemistry and instincts

has me hot and bothered. Besides, I still have those condoms; might as well put them to use. Look, Rea, let me go, so I can get ready."

"Okay, let me know what happens. See you later," Reagan said, and hung up.

Madison tossed the phone on her bed, hopped up and went over to the dresser. She opened the bottom drawer, reached in the back and took out the sexy black La Perla negligee that she didn't get a chance to wear before. She also grabbed the unopened box of condoms, and then closed the drawer. Madison didn't want to raise any suspicions by carrying an overnight bag, so she stuffed the contents into her Marc Jacobs purse. She then showered, put on a pair of Seven jeans, a silk baby-doll top, and cork heel wedges. She spritzed her neck with D&G Light Blue, and left her room.

"Mom!" Madison yelled out, but her mother wasn't at home. *She's probably at the park*, Madison thought. She scribbled a note, telling her mother that she was shopping and would be back before dinner. Madison left the note on the table in the foyer, and dashed out the door.

"You need a taxi, Ms. Reynolds?" asked the doorman.

"Yes, thank you."

"No problem," he said, and then pressed the taxi light in the front of the building. A few minutes later, a yellow cab was pulling up in front.

Madison told the driver Ian's address. On the way there, she took out her compact and dusted her face with some powder. She also smeared her lips with gloss. She rushed out of the house so fast that she didn't get a chance to do her face. By the time she finished sprucing up, they were in front of Ian's building. Madison paid the driver and got out.

"Hey, Beautiful," Ian greeted her, when he opened the door. He then gave her a tight hug, pressing his body close to hers. "Ohh, you feel so good."

Madison hugged him back, and could feel his penis grinding into her groin. Although she wanted to have sex with him, she didn't expect him to come to the door ready and able. "Uh, can a girl at least get a drink before she gets laid?" Madison chuckled, pulling away from him.

"Just one; remember what happened last time," Ian said, referring to her getting drunk and passing out.

"Yeah, I remember, and trust me, I won't be getting wasted today. Now get behind that bar, and fix me a Pomtini!"

"At your service," he said, walking into the living room. Ian fixed them each a drink, and then joined Madison on the couch. "How was Lucas's launch party?"

"It was awesome," she said, sipping her cocktail.

"Man, who knew that the new guy was a budding star? We really had him pegged all wrong."

"You can say that again. He's still pissed about the run-in we had his first day of school."

"How do you know that?"

"Because a photographer wanted to get some pictures

of us last night, and he flat out refused; it was so embarrassing. I've never been dissed in public like that before," Madison told him, with a tinge of sadness in her voice.

Ian put his drink on the cocktail table, and wrapped his arm around Madison. "Oh, baby, don't worry about it. That guy may be a singer, but he'll never have old money like my family has, and if you want to be seen in the social pages of any magazine just say the word. My parents know all the editors on a first-name basis. See, that's the kind of clout that old money will buy. Now forget about being rejected by some fresh-out-of-the-gate singer, and give me a kiss."

Before Madison could say a word, Ian had his tongue down her throat. While he was kissing her, his right hand was roaming underneath her top, and fondling her breasts. Everything was happening so fast that Madison felt her head spinning. "Wait a minute, Ian, slow down," she said, slightly pushing him away.

"What's wrong, baby? Aren't you ready?" he panted.

"Yes, but you're going too fast." Madison picked up her glass and downed her drink.

"No problem. I'll slow down. Maybe another Martini will loosen you up."

"Okay, just one more. While you're fixing drinks, I'm going to your bedroom to change. Give me ten minutes, and then come in. I promise I'll be more than ready," she said, taking her purse off the sofa and heading toward his room.

Ian's room looked more like a high-tech office, than

a bedroom. He had a huge flat-screen Apple computer complete with a webcam on his desk, a printer, and fax machine. Madison set her purse on his desk, so that she could take out her sexy negligee, and as she did, she hit the mouse with her bag and the computer screen went from the screen-saver to a live screen.

"Hey, Big Boy, where did you go?" asked a woman's voice.

Madison looked at the screen, and there was a live webcam picture of a grown woman. Madison stared at the screen, not believing what she was seeing. The woman was topless, and sitting on a bed playing with her breasts.

"Are you there? We were having fun, and you disappeared. Come back so we can finish our striptease game. Look, I paid you for the entire hour, so you'd better hurry back," she said, sounding pissed.

Madison backed away from the computer, so that she wouldn't be caught by the webcam. "What the hell is going on!? No wonder Ian had a hard-on when he came to the door. He was fooling around online!" Madison said, underneath her breath, so that the webcam woman wouldn't hear her. She then grabbed her purse, and headed for the door.

Just as she was exiting his room, Ian was coming in, a martini in each hand. "Hey, where you going?" he asked, looking confused.

"You don't need me. Apparently you already have someone else to play *striptease* with!" she said, looking at him with contempt.

"What are you talking about?"

"Don't play dumb, Ian. Check your computer. Ms. Big Boobs is waiting!" And with that, Madison was out the door before he had a chance to respond.

Madison had automatically assumed that Ian was also a virgin, but she was dead wrong. Not only was he not a virgin, he was a paid porno freak! Talk about keeping secrets!!

37

"Dude, you gotta be shitting me!" PG exclaimed. Ian had called him after Madison stormed out.

"I wish I were kidding."

"Dude, I don't get it. Why would you be operating a porn site? It's not like you need the money."

"It wasn't about the money. I guess I was bored, and…"

"And horny!" PG added.

"Touché. Anyway, I spend so much time alone in the penthouse that I wanted something to do, so I started poking around on the internet. I found this one chat room, where people were talking about operating porn businesses, so I did some investigating, and presto, I'm in business."

"Who are your clients?"

"Mostly lonely housewives. We usually played naughty games, for which I charged by the hour," Ian explained.

"Wow! Aren't you the young Hugh Hefner? So are you going to stay in business?"

"No. Now that Madison knows, it's making me feel sleazy. You should have seen the dirty look she gave me before she left. She looked at me like I was slime. I want to try and redeem myself, plus I don't want the word to get around that I'm into internet porn. If I tainted the Reinhardt name, my parents would probably disinherit me, and I couldn't let that happen."

"I hear you. So, have you talked to Madison since she left?" PG asked.

"No. I've been calling her non-stop, but she keeps sending me to voicemail. I've got to talk to her so that I can explain."

"You're not going to tell her the truth, are you?"

"Yeah, I had planned to. What else can I say? I mean, she saw the naked woman with her own eyes, so it'll be hard for me to lie about it now," Ian said, sounding hopeless.

PG was silent for a moment, and then said. "Tell her it was research."

"Research? What type of research?"

"Tell her that you're helping me with my screenplay. And that I asked you to check out various porn sites. I'm almost finished writing the script, and I can show it to her, so she'll believe you."

"Dude, that's an excellent idea! Wait a minute, is there a porno storyline in the movie? Knowing Madison, she'll want to read the script from the first page to the last," Ian said, making sure that their lie would hold water.

"Yes and no. I mean there's not a porn storyline per se, but there is a lot of sex in the movie, so tell her that you were researching various sexual preferences."

"PG, that's perfect! I can definitely lie my way out of this mess now. Thanks for coming to my rescue. This was a close call. I definitely don't want to lose Madison over getting some cheap thrills. Dude, I really learned my lesson. The next time I'm bored and horny, I'm going to buy a *Playboy*, and some lubricant!"

"That's a good idea."

Getting busted had brought Ian back to reality. He now realized that keeping his girlfriend and his family name intact was more important than cheap thrills.

38

"I can't believe Mr. Bougie Reinhardt is a Porn King!" Reagan exclaimed.

"Please don't call him that," Madison told her.

"*Isn't* he?"

"No! He was never a 'Porn King,' as you so crudely put it. He was doing research for PG."

"When did he give you that load of crap?" Reagan asked cryptically.

"After a dozen or so messages from him, I finally decided to answer his call. Anyway, Ian told me that PG is writing a screenplay, and that he's been doing research for the movie."

"What type of research requires him to entertain naked women on the internet?" Reagan asked, with her eyebrow raised.

"It's a movie about the sexual preferences of upper-echelon teens."

"Hmm, that's interesting. I can't wait to read that script," Reagan said, finally letting up.

"Me either. I told Ian that I have to see the script for

myself before I let him off the hook." Madison and Reagan were in the taxi on the way to Ian's penthouse to peruse the screenplay.

"After you finish, I'm next in line."

"I'm sure they won't have a problem with both of us reading it," Madison said.

"What side of the street do you want?" asked the gruff taxi driver, interrupting their conversation.

"You can pull up in the circular drive, and let us out in front of the door," Madison said, with an air of entitlement.

The driver didn't respond. He did as instructed, and dropped the girls off at the entrance to the multi-billion-dollar residential complex.

"Hey, Beautiful," Ian sang, as he opened the door. He tried to lean in and smooch Madison on the cheek, but she dodged his kiss.

"Ian, you have a long way to go before your lips touch this face again," she said haughtily, and strutted into the penthouse with Reagan following behind.

"Mad, I was only trying to say hi," he said, in an effort to brush off her comment.

"A simple hello will do for now."

"Hey, guys," PG said, once the girls entered the living room. "What's your poison?" he asked, already sipping on a cocktail.

"The usual," they said in unison.

"I got the drinks, dude," Ian told him, and went behind the bar to shake up a couple of Pomtinis.

"Rea, I got something for you," PG said to Reagan.

She instantly started smiling. One of PG's gifts was exactly what the doctor ordered, especially after her ordeal at the launch party. "Oh, PG, what is it?" she asked, sounding like a fifth-grader.

"You'll have to open it and see," he said, handing her a red leather box.

Reagan took one look at the box, and instantly recognized it as Cartier. She frantically opened the lid, and gasped!

"You like it?" PG asked.

"Like it? I love it!" she exclaimed, taking out the signature Love bracelet.

"Omigod! I've always wanted one of those!" Madison squealed, eyeing the gold bracelet.

"And now, you have one!" Ian said, producing a red box of his own, and handing it to Madison.

She looked at the box, and for a millisecond, thought about rejecting the gift. She knew that Ian was trying to buy her forgiveness, and though she was still mad at him, she wanted the bracelet, so she took the box out of his hand and opened it. "Look, Rea, now *we're* twins!" Madison exclaimed, putting on the exact same bracelet.

The girls hugged each other in the middle of the floor, enthralled over their gifts du jour.

While they were gushing over their expensive presents, Ian and PG were giving each other the eye. Their plan to distract the girls was a no-brainer. They knew that when it came down to it, Madison and Reagan were suckers for luxury goods, and would forget all about reading a boring screenplay—which they did.

"Oh, come on, enough with the warm and fuzzies. Let's get wasted!" PG said.

And with that, the four overprivileged teens commenced to drinking the night away, like they had done so many times before. Their worlds revolved around each other, and they could not have cared less about hurting someone's feelings, or finding peace in the Middle East. For now, their perfect world was perfect, but the question was…how long would the fantasy last before their little bubble burst?

39

Kennedy and Roshonda went to their Green Gardens meeting. Afterward, they met Lucas and Devin at the Starbucks on 125th Street.

"Hey, guys," Lucas said, once they came through the door.

"Hey, Lucas." Kennedy smiled. Even though she had seen him the night before, she still enjoyed seeing his handsome face.

"Yo, Kennedy, you sho did look good last night!" Devin said, eyeballing her.

"Man, back off. This is my girl," Lucas said, hugging Kennedy.

Devin threw his hands in the air. "My bad, Dawg."

"So, ladies, what are you drinking?" Lucas asked, once they stepped up to the counter.

Kennedy quickly looked over the menu, and then said. "I'll have a decaf latte with a double shot of hazelnut."

"And I'll have a half decaf, half caf cappuccino with extra whip," Ro said.

"What about you, Man? Whatcha drinking?" Lucas asked Devin.

"Man, I got money. You don't have to buy coffee for me," Devin said, sounding slightly offended.

"Man, I know I don't have to, but I want to, so what do you want?"

Devin rattled off his order, and Lucas bought drinks all around.

Once they were settled in the back of the coffee shop at a table, they began rehashing the party.

"Girl, I'm so sorry that your sister stepped to you like that," Ro said, after Kennedy explained how Reagan had tried to impersonate her in order to steal Lucas away.

"Thanks. I truly wish that Reagan and I were close like sisters are supposed to be. It really hurts that she tried to stab me in the back like that," she said sadly, and hung her head.

Lucas put his arm around her shoulders. "Cheer up, Ken; it's not your problem that she's twisted."

Kennedy lifted her head. "You're right. It's still so hard to believe that we came from the same mother, on the same day."

"I can believe it, 'cuz both of y'all is fine," Devin butted in. He had seen Reagan on her way out, and automatically assumed that it was Kennedy until Lucas told him the story.

They looked at him, and said at the same time, "Shut up!"

"Anyway, sounds like she is so caught up with status, and trying to be on the scene that she'll step on anybody to get there," Ro said.

"Yeah, that pretty much sums it up," Kennedy agreed.

"Hopefully, she and her crew will learn that money only buys you more stuff, and doesn't make you a better person. Also, what you do for a living doesn't make you who you are; just because I have a record out, I'm still the same person. I don't think I'm better than anybody else," Lucas said wisely.

"Unfortunately, that's not how they think. They think that wearing expensive clothes and jewelry puts them above the rest, and being rich makes a person superior," Kennedy said.

"Man, they have a lot to learn. There are so many messed-up rich people in the world. All you have to do is look at the entertainment shows to see that. Some of these stars are drunks, on drugs or have eating disorders. Now if that makes them better than the average person, then let me be average," Lucas added.

"You got that right," Ro agreed. "Anyway, enough about them losers. Lucas, I saw your video on BET! It was dope! I'm so proud of you, boy!!!" Ro said, congratulating him.

"Thanks, Ro. Sorry, I couldn't invite you to the release party. Since it was a small venue, I only had three tickets."

"No prob."

"Trust me; next time you'll definitely be on the list."

"I'ma hold you to it," Ro said.

"So, Ro, you still excited about coming to Walburton next term?" Kennedy asked, switching subjects.

"You know I am! I've already ordered my uniform. I can't wait; it's going to be a blast!" she exclaimed.

"I don't want to burst your bubble, but it's not as exciting as you might think. First of all, the classes are really hard, and secondly, the students are snobs. If you think Reagan and Madison are bad, wait until you run into some of the other overprivileged divas—both male and female. If they're not spending their trust funds like Monopoly money, then they're having wild sex, or so I've heard," Kennedy said, giving Roshonda an earful.

"Well, I don't have anything to worry about 'cuz I ain't got no trust fund to run through, and I don't plan on giving into peer pleasure!" she said, rolling her neck.

"Ro, you are something else!" Kennedy laughed. "I can't wait until next term; it's going to be a whole new world. Not only do I have a boyfriend, but I'm going to have *my* own crew, or should I say my own down-to-earth crew!"

"I'll drink to that," Ro said, raising her cardboard cup.

The four of them toasted with their coffee-based drinks, and hung out the rest of the afternoon like normal teenagers. Kennedy had finally found her niche. She was no longer the odd man out!

about the author

Danita Carter, a Chicago native, is the author of *Murder in the Hamptons* and co-author of *Revenge is Best Served Cold*, *Talk of the Town*, and *Success is the Best Revenge*. In addition to writing, Danita also designs jewelry, and has enjoyed a career on Wall Street with several top financial institutions. Danita currently splits her time between New York and Chicago. For more information, visit her at www.danitacarter.com.

IF YOU ENJOYED "PEER PLEASURE,"
BE SURE TO CHECK OUT

MURDER IN THE HAMPTONS

BY DANITA CARTER
AVAILABLE FROM STREBOR BOOKS

[1]

"Why are all these people still outside? We need to clear out the entire area," Detective Pratt instructed.

"We've been telling everybody to go back inside the boat so that they can be questioned, but they won't go," the police officer said, sounding frustrated.

Detective Pratt stood on the gangplank and looked up at the three-story, multi-million-dollar yacht. There were people peering over the railings from all three decks, staring down into the coal-black water. Detective Pratt knew exactly what was capturing their attention; she had seen it too, the minute she came upon the scene. She looked over at the water again, where police divers were marking off the crime scene with yellow plastic caution strips. She exhaled hard. "Come with me," she told the officer.

The two of them went aboard. "Okay, people, back inside. Nobody goes home until everyone is questioned," Detective Pratt announced to the ogling partygoers.

"Back inside, people. Let's move it," the officer echoed, waving his flashlight like a wand.

Detective Pratt could hear the buzz of whispers as guests eased toward the entrance.

"Oh my God, I can't believe this!"

"It's like something out of a movie."

"Yeah, a horror movie."

They were right. There hadn't been a murder in the Hamptons in quite a while, and when the news broke in the morning, residents would be horrified.

"Who owns this boat?" Detective Pratt asked another officer.

"Liza Lord," he said promptly. Everyone on the island knew that the Lords had the most opulent yacht at the marina. Detective Pratt was new to the island, and wasn't familiar with the Lords.

"Go get her," Detective Pratt said with urgency in her voice.

"Right away," the officer responded, then disappeared into the crowd. A few minutes later, he came back with the owner in tow.

Before speaking, the detective checked out the woman with a discerning eye. Liza Lord was dressed to the hilt in a stark white, silk halter gown, with a thin silver belt wrapped around her slim waist. The belt had tiny rhinestones—or were they diamonds?—encrusted around a square buckle. Large teardrop diamonds were dangling from her earlobes, and her neck and wrists were also dripping in diamonds. Her copper-colored skin was flawless; no wrinkles or any other signs of a stressful life. One look at her, and anyone could see that Ms. Lord came from money; not only a couple of million, but old money that had lasted for generations.

"I understand this is your boat," the detective said.

"Yes, *Lady Lord* is my *yacht*," she said, making the correction obvious.

"Is this an annual party that you give on your boat?" Detective Pratt asked, deliberately using the incorrect term. She hated the upper-crusty tone that rich people used to talk down to common folk, and whenever she could get in a dig, she did.

Liza rolled her eyes and said with a discerning air, "This is not my affair. I merely provided the venue." Liza had been thrilled to help Donovan plan the party, but this nosey detective was pissing her off. That and a dead body had completely soured her mood.

"Then whose party is it?" Detective Pratt snapped.

"Donovan Smart's."

"The rapper?"

"Yes. It's his White and Platinum party, given to introduce himself to the community."

That explains why everyone is dressed in white and silver, the detective thought. "Where is he?"

Liza shrugged her shoulders and then answered, "I don't know."

"Excuse me, Detective, but they're ready to take the body out of the water now," the officer told her.

"Okay, I'll be right there." The detective then turned back to Liza. "Can you hang around for a few minutes? I'd like to ask you some more questions."

"Do I need to call my attorney?"

"That's up to you. My questions are standard and will be quick. We can either do it here, or you *and* your attorney can come down to the station. The choice is yours."

Liza exhaled and thought about the situation for a moment. She wasn't about to be carted down to some godforsaken police station. Besides, she didn't have anything to hide. "Okay, I'll be below deck, in my stateroom," she said, and sauntered away.

Detective Pratt made her way out to the dock. She stood there and watched the divers pull a woman's lifeless body from the water. The woman was also dressed in white and silver; obviously she had been on the guest list. The burning questions now were who was she, and how did she end up floating facedown in the bay? Was it an accidental death, or murder?

The morning after the drowning, Detective Theodora Pratt—Theo for short—pored over her notes. To her amazement, Liza Lord had been extremely cooperative and had filled her in on the major players at the party. There was the host, rapper Donovan Smart, aka TuSmArt; his sister, Reece; and her best friend, Chyna. Also in attendance were Dr. Lars Braxton and his wife, Remi, new money residents of Coco Beach. Troy Hamilton, the chef and owner of Café Coco, was there, as well as a smattering of the old money residents who had summered in that part of the Hamptons for generations.

According to Liza, Donovan had given the party to ingratiate himself into the community. Most of the people who lived in Coco Beach were snobs, and didn't want a rapper disrupting their tranquility. Donovan had wanted to prove to them that he and his crew were house-trained and that there was nothing to be intimidated about. The party had been a success, until someone wound up dead.

"How's it going?" the chief of police asked, coming into her office.

Theo thumped the notes on her desk. "This is going to be an interesting case, to say the least. We have an eclectic cast of characters here. I'm interviewing the rapper, Donovan Smart"—she looked at her watch—"in about ten minutes. After I finish with him, I'm going down the list. I'll probably be here all night." Although she had talked briefly with the guests last night, she wanted more in-depth interviews with some of the key people at the party.

"Okay; let me know how it's shaping up. We're going to need to wrap this case up as soon as possible. The residents will want to know if the woman jumped, accidentally fell overboard, or was pushed. If she was pushed, then it's murder, and Coco Beach hasn't seen a murder in God knows when."

"I'm on it, Chief."

Ten minutes later, right on time, in walked Donovan Smart, looking more like an executive for a Fortune 500 company than a rapper. He was dressed in a navy blue suit, white shirt, and baby-blue tie. The suit fit his brawny frame perfectly, and the white shirt seemed to glow against his chocolate skin.

Donovan Smart's name fit him to a tee. He wasn't merely smart; he was brilliant, a borderline genius. His IQ was right up there with Einstein's. He'd skipped two grades in elementary school and graduated high school when he was only sixteen. His GPA was an astonishing 4.0, and he'd received scholarship offers from Yale, Northwestern, Harvard, and NYU. But to the disappointment of his guidance counselor, he turned down the chance to attend an Ivy League institution, preferring instead to dive deep into his music.

Donovan had been writing rap lyrics since his first taste of the music released by The Notorious B.I.G. The second he heard Christopher Wallace's raspy voice deliver those dope rhythmic lyrics, Donovan was hooked, and knew that he had to be in the rap game.

Unlike the other boys in the neighborhood who hung out playing b-ball all day and night, Donovan would sequester himself in his bedroom, writing songs. He saved enough cash from a part-time job dropping fries at Mickey-D's to buy a keyboard and a secondhand sound system, complete with CD burner and microphone. He set up a makeshift studio in his room and would work on tunes for hours on end, until he had the right track to accompany his words. His songs were profound. He wrote of growing up in a crack-infested neighborhood, where the habit-forming synthetic drug had grandmothers selling their bodies to get a ten-dollar hit. He wrote of teenage mothers struggling to work *and* finish school so they could move out of the 'hood to provide a better life for their children. He wrote of witnessing shootouts and seeing the bullet-riddled bodies of his peers; their young lives snuffed out like insignificant, flickering flames right before his eyes. By the time Donovan had graduated from high school, he had a vast catalogue of work, and was ready to make some noise in the world of music.

Initially, he wanted to be a writer/producer, but he couldn't find anyone with a unique-enough vibe to record his demo. Everybody he auditioned tried to sound like Tupac, Biggie, or Ice Cube. Though each was great in his own right, he wanted originality, not a remix of the classics. Tired of wasting time with wannabes, he went into the studio and laid the tracks himself. To his astonishment, he realized that he possessed within himself the unique sound that he craved.

With the demo complete, Donovan was ready to shop for that elusive record deal. However, he knew from reading trade magazines and watching celebrity profiles on television that it often took years to sign with a major label. He couldn't fathom the idea of wasting his energy running down an A&R exec to get a contract that only paid pennies on the dollar.

Instead of taking the traditional route, he opted to go underground and shave years off the conventional process. He made mass copies—since he owned the music there were no copyright issues—and sold his CDs on the street, keeping one hundred percent of the profit. Donovan couldn't produce the music fast enough. The neighborhood was hooked. His dope rap was the new crack! The message in his lyrics transcended age, touching young and old alike. People would line up outside his apartment door to buy the homemade discs.

It didn't take long for the big boys to come a-callin' once they heard the *ka-ching* of a proven money-making machine. In the music industry (as with all industries), the name of the game was profit with a capital "P." After selling more than fifty thousand CDs in less than a year, Donovan had proven without a doubt that his music was indeed profitable.

The marketing team at Lysten UP Records reasoned that if he could generate a loyal following without the benefit of corporate dollars behind him, then he would surely go platinum with their worldwide distribution propelling him into the stratosphere and beyond. Lysten UP wooed Donovan with SUVs on d.u.b.s., bling, phat gear, and a fat advance check when he signed on the dotted line. Since he'd brought a proven track record to the table, his attorney was able to negotiate top-notch terms in his contract, including creative control for the artist, which was rare for a neophyte.

Six platinum albums and a Brink's truck of cash later, Donovan was the new prince of hip-hop. Though music would always be his first love, he decided to branch out and diversify his dollars in several different arenas. Following the lead of Sean Combs—whom Donovan admired and had studied in the press long before Donovan made his millions—Donovan started his own clothing line—SmArtGeAr. He followed that with a restaurant, simply called Donovan's. And he partnered with real estate mogul Donald Trump to open a trendy boutique hotel in Harlem. Professionally, his life couldn't get much better. He was amassing a vast empire, had three singles on *Billboard*'s Top 20 simultaneously, and was co-producer on another two top singles.

On the flip side, his personal life—or more to the point, his love life—was stagnant. He wrote ballads of unrequited love, but had never experienced the blood-rushing, adrenaline-pumping thrill of giving his heart to a woman.

One of New York's most eligible bachelors, Donovan had a smorgasbord of women at his disposal, from video dancers, to models, to Grammy Award–winning singers. As alluring as they all were, he wanted something more. He didn't only want a woman with killer looks. He wanted brains as part of the package. However, the three "B"s—beauty, body, and brains—was a tough combination to find among the women in his circle.

To save face and to keep his fans satiated with the juicy details of his so-called escapades, his publicist arranged, on occasion, dates with some of Broadway's leading actresses. This media tactic was used to solidify his image as the consummate ladies' man, but in reality, Donovan was as lonely as a castaway on a deserted island.